D0426552

Biggie
and the
Quincy
Ghost

Biggie
and the
Quincy
Ghost

Nancy Bell

Thomas Dunne Books / St. Martin's Minotaur ❧ New York

THOMAS DUNNE BOOKS.
An imprint of St. Martin's Press.

BIGGIE AND THE QUINCY GHOST. Copyright © 2001 by Nancy Bell.
All rights reserved. Printed in the United States of America.
No part of this book may be used or reproduced in any manner
whatsoever without written permission except in the case of
brief quotations embodied in critical articles or reviews.
For information, address St. Martin's Press,
175 Fifth Avenue, New York, N.Y. 10010.

www.minotaurbooks.com

Library of Congress Cataloging-in-Publication Data

Bell, Nancy.
    Biggie and the Quincy ghost / Nancy Bell.—1st ed.
      p. cm.
    ISBN 0-312-26560-3
      1. Biggie (Fictitious character : Bell)—Fiction. 2. Women detectives—
Fiction. 3. Grandmothers—Fiction. 4. Texas—Fiction. I. Title.

PS3552.E5219 B57 2001
813'.54—dc21
                                                                2001037193

First Edition: September 2001

10 9 8 7 6 5 4 3 2 1

Acknowledgments

This book would not exist without the ever-so-tactful comments from the Shoal Creek Writers: Karen Fitzjerrall, Dena Garcia, Eileen Joyce, Sharon Kahn, and Judy Austin Mills, who have been with me every step of the way. It is their keen instincts and unwavering insistence on excellence that send me back to the keyboard again and again until what I produce meets their strict standards.

I would like to thank Elissa R. Ballesteros of the Austin Public Library for taking the time to locate a recipe for Willie Mae's Lane cake, the original having been lost. It was a great help, although it must be admitted that Willie Mae insisted on adding a few touches of her own before she would permit it to be printed.

I would especially like to acknowledge my wonderful agent, Vicky Bijur, who goes not only the second mile, but the third, fourth, and as far as it takes to get the job done.

Also, and this is long past due, I thank Ruth Cavin, my editor at St. Martin's Press, who has taught me more than she will ever know.

Finally, thanks to the citizens of Jefferson, Texas, from whose town and its history I have borrowed freely in the creation of the fictional town of Quincy. However, I hasten to add that the characters in this story were born in my mind and exist only on the pages of this book.

Biggie and the Quincy Ghost

Job's Jottings from Julia

July 24   Well, the Independence Day holiday has come and gone, and this reporter is glad of it. The noise around this town would drive a preacher to take a drink. DeWayne Boggs blew his right eyebrow off with a Roman candle and had to be taken to the Center Point hospital for stitches. DeWayne stated that he was looking into the business end of the rocket because he wanted to see the ball of fire come out. DeWayne's mother, Mrs. Betty Jo Darling, states that DeWayne will be back on the baseball diamond next week playing right field for the Little League Dodgers. When questioned further, she stated that it didn't much matter whether he could see or not, because the ball never makes it to right field anyway.

Butch Hickley of Hickley's House of Flowers states that the fall bedding plants have come in, but you'd better

1

get them early as the Almanac says we're in for an early frost this year.

It appears that the town is not to have a historical society after all. An exploratory committee headed by Biggie Weatherford has just returned from a trip to Quincy where the members had hoped to pick up some pointers from the Quincy Historical Society. However, the meetings were called off due to a shocking murder that occurred at the very hotel where the committee was staying. The committee is now looking into other avenues for improving the cultural life of our citizens. Stay tuned.

1

My name is J.R. Weatherford. I'm twelve and a half years old, and I live in Job's Crossing, Texas, with my grandmother, Biggie, who is called Biggie because when I was little I couldn't say "Big Momma," and Rosebud and Willie Mae, who live in their own little house in our backyard. I have a new puppy, Bingo. Bingo is in trouble right now because this morning he went to the bathroom in Biggie's underwear drawer. If you ask me, she shouldn't be leaving her drawers open with a puppy around, but I could tell she wasn't in the mood to listen to reason, so I didn't press it. Now, Biggie is making Bingo live outside for an indefinite period of time.

I have lived in a big white house in Job's Crossing, Texas, with Biggie since I was six years old. Before that, I lived in Dallas with my daddy, who sold porta-potties to construction sites, and my mama, who is susceptible to sick headaches and spends a lot of time in bed with the shades drawn. She says the only thing that will help is Miller Beer. My daddy died after an I beam fell on the Porta-Potti he was setting up. Mama said it was just like Royce not to leave her one cent of insurance. That's why she had to take a job at the Autotel Ballroom on Harry Hines Boulevard. When Biggie, who was my daddy's mother, heard that, she said she was not going to have any grandson of hers raised by a person who served drinks in a cheap dive, so she got in her car and drove to Dallas to bring me home. Mama didn't argue hardly at all.

Me and Rosebud were out in the yard building a pen for Bingo when Biggie came trotting down the back steps with a letter in her hand. She was smiling, so I guess she'd forgotten about being mad.

"Surprise," she said, "we're all going to Quincy next weekend, for four whole days!"

"Well, now, ain't that nice," Rosebud said, taking out his handkerchief and mopping the sweat off his face with his big black hand. "You folks deserve a little break."

"Oh, you'll get to go too, honey." Biggie patted her hair. "I need you to drive."

Rosebud's face fell. "I don't know, Miss Biggie. I was plannin' on paintin' the garage next weekend."

Biggie continued as if he'd never said a word. "You see, the Quincy Historical Society is having a weekend workshop on how to preserve history in a small town, and they have invited our officers to attend."

Biggie is a Very Important Person in Job's Crossing on account of she is the richest person in town, and her family has been here the longest. She decided to organize a historical society after we took a trip to Williamsburg, Virginia, last Christmas. Biggie figured Job's Crossing could cash in on its glorious history the same way Williamsburg was doing. Her idea was that Job's Crossing has existed under the flags of six different countries, while Williamsburg could only claim three. When I pointed out to her about how we learned in history class that there wasn't even a town here when the French and Spanish first settled Texas, she said it didn't matter, because there certainly were Indians here, and she wasn't going to be a racist and ignore that fact.

"Biggie, I don't want to go to Quincy. I was planning to camp out Saturday night." I was ready to go into whining mode if she said I had to go.

Biggie read my mind and gave me a look. "Of course you're going," she said. "You can learn a lot on this trip. Besides, J.R., you know how you love history. My sakes, they have about four museums in that little town. Not to mention the fact that the hotel we'll be staying in is a museum in itself—and it has a ghost!"

"Ooo-wee," I said. "For real?" She's right, I do like history, but I like ghost stories even better.

"For real," Biggie said. "They tell about it right here in this brochure they sent. You can read it tonight after supper. Right now, I've got to go in and call the other officers so they can make arrangements for the trip."

After I watched Biggie scurry back inside the house, I turned to the big black man beside me. "Rosebud, do you believe in ghosts?"

Rosebud was pouring concrete around a post he'd just set. "Sure do," he said, not looking up.

5

I sat on the ground and watched him pour. I watched his big arm muscles move under the white tee shirt he wore. "I'll bet you know a story about a ghost." Rosebud has a story for just about everything that happens.

"Nope," Rosebud said, standing up and stretching his back. "Hand me that posthole digger over there. I gotta make this next one a little deeper."

Rosebud is my best friend in the whole world. He has little gold hearts, clubs, diamonds, and spades built right into his four front teeth. He won them off a dentist in a crap game down in New Orleans. Rosebud tells wonderful stories; some I believe, some I don't, but I wouldn't tell him that because they are very interesting, even if untrue.

By the time we finished the pen and came in the house, Willie Mae had supper on the table. She turned from the counter where she was stirring sugar into a pitcher of iced tea and waved her spoon at us. "Git in there and wash up. Supper's getting cold."

Personally, I couldn't see what was getting cold. We had cold sliced ham, cold potato salad, cold sliced tomatoes and cucumbers from the garden, fresh-baked zucchini bread, and iced tea. But you don't argue with Willie Mae, who is a voodoo lady and can turn you into a frog in a blue-eyed minute, if she takes the notion. She came to live with us when I was just a kid and me and Biggie were trying to keep house all by ourselves and not doing a very good job of it. I'll never forget the day she came carrying all her things in a black satin pillowcase. Our last maid, Codella, had gone running down the street screaming her head off the day before just because she happened to find a catfish swimming in Biggie's toilet. It wasn't anything to get excited about. Biggie had just put him in there to keep him fresh until she had time to clean him. I have to admit, though, the house was a mess. Willie Mae didn't waste any time taking down all the drapes and shaking the dust off them, cleaning out the pantry, airing all the bed linens, waxing the floors—well, you get the picture. In no time our house was spic-and-span and the good smells of Willie Mae's cooking had filled the kitchen. Not long after Willie Mae had moved into the little house out back, Rosebud got out of jail in Mansfield, Louisiana, and he moved in, too.

We had just sat down in the kitchen to eat when in walked Butch, our town florist. Some people think Butch is a little strange just because he dresses funny and talks like a girl. Personally, I like Butch. Live and let live, is what I say. Mattie and Norman Thripp who own Mattie's Tea Room down on the square came in right behind him. Miss Mattie is round and soft and has blue hair. She wears floaty dresses with big flowers on them. She and Mr. Thripp have only been married two years even though they are both pretty old. Biggie says Norman Thripp had as much chance as a grasshopper in a chicken yard once Mattie set her cap for him. She also says Mattie leads him around by the nose, which I don't understand. His nose is little and mashed in. If she said she led him around by the ears, that I could understand. He has ears like a monkey, and they stick straight out. His eyes look like ball bearings.

"The door was open so we just came on in," Miss Mattie said, walking right up to the table. "Umm, ham. Is that ham from the farm?"

She meant Biggie's family farm out south of town,

where Biggie was raised. Now the Sontags live there. For rent, they pay Biggie a dollar a year and all the fresh food we can eat. Their daughter, Monica, is bald on one side of her head from being left too close to the fire when she was a baby. She is not afraid of anything and is my second-best friend next to Rosebud.

Biggie nodded. "There's plenty," she said. "Why don't you pull up a chair and join us?"

They didn't waste any time. Before you could say Jack Robinson, they had gone into the dining room and were dragging chairs in and squeezing them around the table.

Willie Mae got up and put three more plates and sets of silverware on the table, then she took three cloth napkins out of the drawer of the pine hutch. Biggie took down three glasses from the cabinet and filled them with iced tea.

"Well, Biggie," Butch said, spearing a slice of ham off the platter. "We're all *so* excited about our little trip to Quincy. I just love that town—so many cute little shops and restaurants. You know, I've got a good friend that runs the Gilded Lily Tea Room right down on Main Street. Umm, this potato salad is good. What you got in it, Willie Mae?"

"Homemade mayonnaise," Willie Mae said. "Don't never use that stuff from the store."

"Well, you ought to bottle the stuff and sell it," Mr. Thripp said, talking with his mouth full. "If you ever want to do it, I'll be glad to go in partners with you."

"Humph." Willie Mae wasn't about to go into business with Mr. Thripp, who will steal the pennies off a dead man's eyes.

"Ruby Muckleroy can't go with us," Miss Mattie said. "You know, Meredith Michelle has taken to teaching twirling lessons to the little girls, and she's having her first recital next weekend. Ruby's been bragging all over town about what a smart businesswoman Meredith Michelle's turned out to be."

Butch got up to pour himself some more tea from the pitcher on the drain board. "Ruby's full of library paste," he said. "Meredith Michelle couldn't even make change when she was working for me last summer. That girl's got talcum powder for brains."

"I guess it will just be the four of us then," Biggie said. "Plus J.R. and Rosebud, of course."

After the others left, I hung around the kitchen and helped Willie Mae with the dishes.

"What will you do without us to take care of, Willie Mae?" I asked.

Willie Mae looked down at me, and for a minute there, I thought she was going to smile. "Reckon I'll think of something," she said. "You left a spot on this one."

I took the glass from her and rubbed it hard with my dishtowel. "Willie Mae," I said, "do you believe in ghosts?"

"Um-hmm."

"Are you scared of um?"

"They just like you and me—they's good ghosts and then they's sorry ghosts."

I picked up a plate to dry. "What do the sorry ones do? Go around scaring people?"

"Worse than that," she said. And that's all she'd say, even though I had about a million more questions to ask.

I went into the den and sat down on Biggie's easy chair next to the fireplace to read the brochure from the hotel. It only had a few lines about the ghost. Most of it was telling about all the famous people who had stayed there. From the pictures, I could see that they had the whole place crammed full of antique furniture and paintings and stuff. I decided then and there that it was going to be a very boring weekend. I was wrong.

Rosebud came in just then and told me he was going out to the front porch to smoke his cigar. I followed him out.

Rosebud propped his feet up on the porch rail and looked up at the full moon peeking down through the oak leaves. "Puts me in mind of the West Monroe Werewolf," he said.

"Tell about it, Rosebud."

"Odie Dell Isom, was his name. Nicest feller you'd ever hope to meet until the full moon come along." Rosebud laughed without making a sound and slapped his knee.

"I don't see what's so funny."

"You would if you knew Odie Dell. He cut hair down at the Spit 'n Polish Tonsorial Emporium on South River Street in West Monroe, Louisiana. Little bitty feller, kinda portly, doncha know. But, oh, boy, when that moon come full, he'd grow a good foot and sprout hair all over his body."

"Did you ever see him do that?"

"Well, not what you'd call with my own eyes, but I did talk to a feller that did. He said old Odie's eyes would get bloodred and he'd sprout big old fangs that hung out over his lips."

"Wow!"

"Odie wouldn't bother folks too much when he had one of his spells, he'd just go out in the creek bottom and howl at the moon. Onc't he scared the water out of Miz Reverend Billups when she come up on him while she was gatherin' hickory nuts."

"And that's all he did?"

"Just about, except that one time."

"What one time was that?"

"Well, old Odie, he was right sweet on Miss Shaunista Timpson, who would tip the scales right around three hundred, or thereabouts. Remember, Odie was just a little feller."

I nodded.

"Miss Shaunista lived with her momma and her two aunties who were also large ladies much like she was. Well, they weren't too keen on Shaunista going off and marrying Odie on account of him bein' such a little shrimp. Besides, she did most of the work around the place while them three just sat around watching soap operas on TV."

"Kinda like Cinderella?"

"I reckon. So every time Odie would come around to take her out, they would all come out on the front porch and cuss at him something awful. Odie told the fellers down at the barbershop that he didn't mind the cussin' too much, but now they'd taken to chunkin' rocks at him." Rosebud tossed his cigar butt over the porch rail. "Why don't you run in the house and pour me a glass of buttermilk?"

Rosebud always does that to me just when the story is

getting good. I hurried back and handed him the buttermilk. "Go on," I begged. "I bet he turned into a werewolf and killed them all."

"Huh? Odie? Naw. He just kept takin' it, and takin' it until he couldn't take it no longer. He says to Miss Shaunista, he says, 'How come your mama and your aunties don't like me?' And she says, 'It's 'cause you be such a little shrimp of a feller. The men in our family has always been big, strappin' men.' Well, Odie went home and thought about that. He thought and he thought, until finally he come up with an idea. The first thing he done was, he went over to the haberdashery store and bought himself a suit about three sizes too big for him. Then he picked out a shirt and some big old shoes."

"I know what's coming."

"Maybe you do, and maybe you don't. Odie knew he was takin' a chance, but he figured if he dressed himself up and came callin' on a full-moon night, he could go as a werewolf and maybe Shaunista's family would like him. Because, lord knows, on them nights, he was certainly a big strappin' feller. He knew he'd have to be on his best behavior though. Sometimes, werewolves don't have real good manners. So Odie puts on his big old clothes and sets out just about sundown. It was a good three miles over to her place. Well, there he goes, shufflin' down the road in his big old shoes and draggin' his pants legs in the dust. Long about the time he clears the woods and comes up to Shaunista's front gate, here comes the moon and, lo and behold, Odie's chest fills out and his legs and arms get longer. Hair sprouts all over him, and his eyes turn red as a baboon's butt."

"Wow, I'd like to see that."

"Be quiet and let me tell this. So here come's the momma and the aunties all ready to start shoutin' cuss words and chunkin' rocks at Odie. When they see him their mouths drop open on account of Odie looks so fine in his new clothes. It don't bother them one bit that he seems like he might could use a shave. Shaunista runs out and takes him by the arm and leads him into the house. He sets a spell, and they offer him sweet potato pie and coffee. Odie controls himself and don't growl once. He figures once he's out in the woods, he can howl at the moon 'til the cows come home. Well, at the end of the evening, he bids um all a good night and leaves. Shaunista's family all congratulate her and tell her how they're glad she's finally found herself a real man."

"So he pulled it off?"

"Almost."

"What does that mean?"

"Wellsir, every morning after breakfast, Shaunista's momma used to come out and throw the slop to her prize layin' hens. She was more than proud of them hens. Ever year, they'd win her a blue ribbon at the parish fair. Well, this particular mornin' she came out, took one look, throwed her apron over her head, and run back in the house screamin' like the devil was after her."

"Oooh! What was it?"

"It was her hens. They was all layin' there in a row in front of the back steps, and each one of um had their heads bit clean off. Old Odie, he just couldn't hold it in for one more second."

"Uh-oh. So, then what happened?"

"Oh, Odie and Shaunista, they got married and moved to the next county, and they never seen her mama and her mean old sisters again."

"That was a good story, Rosebud. How did Odie get to be a werewolf in the first place?"

"That's a whole 'nother story, and it's mighty late. You get on up to bed, and maybe I'll tell it to you another time."

That night, lying in bed, I thought about all that had happened to me since I was six years old and was sent to live with Biggie. I'd been thrown in a dark hole, kidnapped by some fake army men, and almost gotten hauled off to Montana to live with my evil other grandmother, but I'd never come up against a real ghost before. Still, I was pretty sure that with Biggie there, nothing really bad could happen. I've never yet seen a situation she couldn't handle.

You might think I dreamed about ghosts and werewolves that night, but I didn't. I had a good night's sleep and dreamed about my puppy playing in his new pen. It's a good thing, too, since once we got to Quincy, I didn't get much rest at all.

2

Biggie got a good deal on a car this year. She bought it from the undertaker over in Center Point, whose business had been so good he decided to upgrade his fleet of limousines. He sold her a Lincoln with very low mileage for a good price. He told her it had never been driven more than twenty miles an hour and I believe him, because did you ever see a funeral procession going faster than that? Since it has a jump seat in the back, Biggie decided Rosebud could drive us all over to Quincy in it even though we might be a little crowded.

The town of Quincy is only thirty-five miles from Job's Crossing, but the two towns are not one bit alike. Rosebud says that's because Quincy is just a hop, skip, and a jump from the Louisiana line and that makes it more Southern, while Job's Crossing is pure-dee Texas. I could see what he meant. The further east we went, the taller the pine

15

trees grew, and the thicker. Occasionally I saw a little Spanish moss hanging from the oak trees.

"We should stop and gather some of that moss," Butch said. "It's just the best thing in the world to use in dried arrangements."

"That's right, we should," Miss Mattie said. "You can buy the stuff at Wal-Mart, but it costs a mint for a little-bitty bag, and it's all dried up, too. Stop the car, Rosebud."

"Maybe we'll stop on the way back," Biggie said, turning in her seat to face Miss Mattie and Butch. "Business before pleasure."

"Once, I made a wreath to go over the mantel at the Masonic Lodge," Butch said. "It had deer horns all over it, and a big bunch of turkey feathers at the top. I just *festooned* that wreath with Spanish moss."

"Humph," Mr. Thripp said. "I'll bet they gypped you on the cost. Those Masons will get in your pocket every chance they get."

"Norman, where did you ever get an idea like that?" Miss Mattie glared at him. "My daddy was a Mason, and I happen to know for a fact that they're very honest. It says somewhere in their secret ritual that they have to be or they can get excommunicated."

"Well, I don't know so much about that," Butch said. "They tell that Lee Harvey Oswald was a Mason—or was he an Elk? I always get those two mixed up."

Miss Mattie spoke up. "I don't think he was either...."

"Look," Biggie interrupted. "There's the city limit sign."

As Rosebud turned the car off the highway and onto

Sweetgum Street, I noticed on either side of us some old Victorian houses. They were painted all different colors, not just white like we have in Job's Crossing, and it seemed that every single one of them had some kind of historical marker stuck up by the door. Old trees lined the sidewalks and came together in the middle of the street. Miss Mattie and Butch were just oohing and aahing over those houses until it would make you sick.

"Look at that nice Queen Anne," Miss Mattie said. "My Law, those oleanders must be eighty years old. Look at the size of them!"

"Um-hum." Butch turned around to look. "Personally, I'd have painted it a nice pink with peach trim and white gingerbread. Brown is just so ordinary."

"See that house on the right with the tower on top?" Biggie pointed. "That's the House of the Epiphany. Stop, Rosebud, so we can see." She pointed to the tower. "If you look close, you can see the three wise men on their camels done in stained glass in the top windows. A bishop built it back in the 1890s. It's only lighted during the Christmas season."

"Hey, look," Butch said, pointing to a pale green house. "That one has a widow's walk."

"Where's the hotel?" I asked, not expecting much because I'd already seen a picture of it on the brochure.

"It's right downtown," Biggie said. "Turn here, Rosebud."

Rosebud stopped for a red light, then made a right turn, and there we were in the middle of the business district. The streets were made of brick and were lined with gift shops, antique shops, little cafes, and dress shops. I

17

wondered where a person would go if they had to buy groceries or a hammer and nails. I didn't see a single store that sold anything anyone would really need. I started to say that when Rosebud slowed the car and stopped in front of the hotel. It wasn't anything but an old two-story square building right on Main Street with a balcony upstairs and rocking chairs out front on the sidewalk. A fancy iron rail surrounded the balcony, and pots of green plants stood on each side of the big front door.

Biggie and Miss Mattie and I went in while Rosebud and Mr. Thripp took the bags out of the car. It was cool and dark inside, and it took a minute for my eyes to adjust so I could look around. The first thing I saw was a bunch of people sitting around in the lobby, which was furnished with (what else?) antiques. A huge rug covered the worn-down wood floor. It was pale green with big pink and yellow roses in a design around the edge and in the middle. Here and there were chairs and sofas covered in shiny material. They didn't look one bit comfortable to me. Pale green velvet drapes with gold fringe covered the tall windows, and next to the curving stairway I saw a statue of a woman holding a basket of cherries. In the center of the room stood a carved round table that held the biggest flower arrangement I'd ever seen. Butch went over and touched the flowers. "They're real!" he said.

Biggie went straight to the registration desk just to the right of the front door. It looked like an old-timey bar out of a Western movie. Behind it was a huge mirror with a wide gold frame. A white-haired lady with a sweet face left the group of people and stepped behind the desk. She wore a light-colored skirt and a blue sweater that exactly matched her eyes. She shook Biggie's hand. "Welcome," she said, "I'm Mary Ann Quincy, manager of the hotel. I'm also a member of the historical society, so you'll be seeing a lot of me. And you must be the famous Biggie Weatherford."

"Me?" Biggie turned pink. "I'm not famous. I'm just..."

"Ah, but you are," Mary Ann interrupted her. "You're well known all over east Texas, not only for your work with the Daughters of the Republic of Texas, but for your detecting skills. We've heard all about how you're always two jumps ahead of the lawmen when it comes to solving murders."

Biggie had recovered her cool. "Well," she said, "I do what I can."

"Are there TVs in the rooms?" I asked without much hope.

"There is in your room." Miss Mary Ann's blue eyes twinkled. "Video games, too. I put it there just for you. It belongs to my son, Brian, but he's in college now and doesn't use it much anymore." She winked at me.

I breathed a sigh of relief and grinned up at her. At least I wouldn't be totally bored this weekend. As it turned out, I didn't have too much time to hang out in my room, and I sure as heck wasn't bored.

While Biggie registered, I looked around. The most interesting thing I spotted was a long table on one side of the room covered with a white cloth. I saw a silver tea service on one end and a bunch of plates full of little-bitty sandwiches and cookies and stuff. My stomach rumbled, and that reminded me; I hadn't had a bite to eat since lunch. I hoped they were planning to share some of that food with us. I wasn't disappointed.

"We have arranged a little tea for you," the white-haired lady said, coming out from behind the desk. "Would you like to see your rooms first?"

Everybody but Rosebud must have been hungry, too, because they all said they'd rather have tea first, then go up to their rooms. Rosebud decided to have a little stroll around town. Miss Mary Ann Quincy led us all into the lobby and began introducing the society members.

"This is Henrietta Lester, but we all call her Hen," she said, looking at a thin woman wearing a black pantsuit and pearls around her neck. Her hair was pinkish red, and even I could tell she was wearing way too much makeup. When she stuck out her hand to shake, I noticed she had rings on dern near every finger. She touched fingers with the Thripps and Biggie, but when Butch came up to shake, she jerked her hand back like she'd been stung. I guess I forgot to mention, Butch was wearing his black satin jeans, fluffy shirt, and black sequined tennies. Butch just grinned and turned to face the person next to her.

This was a man, and he was old—I mean really old, older than Biggie, even older than Biggie's Aunt Bill Wooten, who lives at the rest home and has to be tied in her wheelchair. But when he stood up to greet the ladies, he was spry as a squirrel and his eyes were just as bright and curious. He wore a pale blue seersucker suit and I saw a Panama hat and a black cane resting beside his chair. Miss Mary Jane introduced him as Lucas Fitzgerald, a lawyer and lifelong resident of Quincy.

"Lucas lives with us here at the hotel," she said.

"Charmed, ladies," Lucas said, actually bowing low to each of them. "And Brother Thripp. Welcome to our town!" Then he stroked his mustache and looked down at me. "And who might our youngest visitor be?"

"I'm J.R. Weatherford, and I'm her grandson," I said pointing to Biggie.

He leaned down and whispered in my ear. "How did they rope you into coming along?"

I shrugged.

"Oh, J.R.'s very interested in history," Biggie piped up.

"That right?" Lucas said, still looking at me.

"Yes, sir."

"Then we'll find plenty for you to do. Yes-siree. How'd you like to help me catalog some papers for the museum tomorrow?"

"Sure," I said, although I wasn't sure just what that meant.

"Then meet me there at two. It's just across the street. Mary Ann can show you where."

Suddenly, I saw a shadow fall over the rug as the biggest woman I'd ever seen stood up from the sofa and took a step toward us, leaning on an ivory-topped walking stick. Her grayish hair was thin and cut like a man's and she had black hair on her arms, which were brown like she'd been working out in the yard a lot. She wore a navy blue dress with a dingy white collar. It fitted her like a tent. She had the look of a person that would rather be outside any old day than attending teas with the ladies.

"Welcome!" she boomed at us. "I'm Alice LaRue, president of this here little organization. The only reason they let me in is because the family I married into has been here

21

longer than anybody else's." When she laughed, the teacups on the table rattled. She reached around behind her and pointed to a mousy girl sitting on the couch. "This here's my daughter, Emily Faye. She keeps the minutes."

The secretary stood up and gave us all a limp hand-shake, looking up at us through her thick glasses. She was wearing a shapeless floweredy dress and had on white tennis shoes. I guessed she must be around eighteen, but the way she was dressed, you'd have thought she was forty.

"Fine," Alice LaRue bellowed. "Now that we've all met, let's head for the tea table. Em, you set at the head and pour out the tea." She stomped over to the table that was just chock-full of goodies. The rest of us followed. "Lordy mercy, would you look at this spread." She looked at Mary Ann. "You do all this yourself?"

"No way." Mary Ann looked over her shoulder from where she'd been prodding Biggie to be first in line. "Annabeth Baugh has been helping me out this summer. She did most of it. I declare, I don't know where that girl learned to do things so nice growing up the way she did."

I'd been eyeballing a silver tray full of little baby pecan pies and thinking I could eat three or four of those. I looked up at Mary Ann. "How did she grow up?"

"Oh, well, hon, she was raised out at Caddo Lake—right next to the bayou. Her folks never had much, that's all."

"Didn't they eat?"

"J.R., that's enough," Biggie said. "What Mary Ann means is, Annabeth never had much chance to cook fancy party food. Here." She handed me a plate, and I headed for the pecan pies.

"Well, I wouldn't say that exactly. She helped me out a little last summer. Where is Annabeth, anyway?" Hen Lester's eyes darted around the room as she picked up a cucumber sandwich and put it on her plate. "I thought she'd be here helping you serve."

Mary Ann was sitting at the other end of the table serving up cream puffs filled with fresh strawberries and whipped cream. "I gave her the afternoon off," she said, not looking at Hen. "She's gone off somewhere with Brian." She plopped a cream puff on Butch's plate, smiling up at him.

Alice LaRue had already gone back to the sofa with her plate. "You'd better keep a sharp eye on that situation," she shouted. "I saw them to driving past my house, and honey, she was practically settin' in the boy's lap."

"It's only a summer romance," Mary Ann said. "Brian's going back to SMU in the fall. He's practically engaged to a nice girl from Dallas. I don't think Annabeth harbors any unrealistic expectations."

"Honey, she's a female, ain't she?" Alice plopped a whole cream puff in her mouth then talked around it. "We're all just naturally prone to expectations. It's in our genes."

After everybody had gotten their food and taken seats, balancing their plates on their knees, the front door opened and the prettiest girl I'd ever seen walked in. She had yellow hair that fell down her back in shiny waves. Her face was tanned a golden brown, and her eyes were as blue as a robin's egg. She wore real short white shorts and a halter top the color of her eyes. Her legs were long and brown and she was wearing white sandals. My eyes must have bugged right out of my head, because Butch punched me and grinned. A boy that I figured must have been Brian because he walked over and kissed Mary Ann on the cheek followed her. He was wearing shorts and a tee shirt and a baseball cap with *Mustangs* printed on the front.

"Come here, you two," Alice LaRue bellowed. "Meet our out-of-town guests."

The two came over and stood before our group while Mary Ann made the introductions. "Where have y'all been?" she asked.

"We went boating on the lake," Brian said. "Hey, Mom, could you spare Annabeth for a little while longer? I want to take her to the dance at the pavilion tonight."

"I don't have to go if you need me," Annabeth said.

"Well, I do need you to help with dinner." Mary Ann smiled at the girl. "Would eight o'clock be too late to go?"

"That would be great, Mom. I'll help." Brian took Annabeth by the arm. "Come on, I've got something to show you in my room." He winked at her.

As those two walked away, I saw Emily Faye look at them with the saddest eyes I'd ever seen on anyone. She saw me looking and quickly built a little smile on her face and asked if anyone wanted any more tea.

After refreshments were over, the group offered to give us a tour of the hotel.

"That would be lovely," Biggie said, and Miss Mattie agreed. Rosebud, who had just come back from his walk, said he had to take the car down to be checked because he'd heard a funny noise driving over, and Mr. Thripp said he'd heard it, too, and he'd be glad to go along to help. I didn't believe that for a minute, but I offered to go

24

and help, too, because I wasn't any more interested in touring the hotel than they were. Of *course* Biggie said I *had* to stay with her. Sometimes I get tired of being treated like a little kid. I'm going on thirteen for gosh sake, but go tell Biggie that.

The first thing they did was lead us over to a big glass-covered case that stood on fat legs like an old piano. Inside, the old hotel register sat on a velvet cushion.

"Normally, we don't take this out of the case. It's priceless." Hen Lester took a small key out of her pocket. "But for you, we will, so you can see for yourselves what a distinguished clientele this place used to have."

I couldn't help thinking how much this woman reminded me of Mrs. Muckleroy back in Job's Crossing.

She raised the glass. Lucas Fitzgerald reached in and gently lifted the giant ledger out, then she closed it. He set it down on the top and began turning the pages. "Gather around. Can you all see?"

We grouped ourselves around the table and peered at the pages.

"Look." He pointed with one long finger at a name. "Ulysses S. Grant, June 16, 1866." The ladies oohed and aahed. "And here." He turned some more pages, pointing to more names. Rutherford B. Hayes, Alma Gluck, Harry Houdini, Oscar Wilde.

"Oscar Wilde?" Butch squeaked. "Oscar Wilde stayed here?"

"He stayed in the Orchid Room," Miss Mary Ann said. "And that's where you're staying, Butch."

"I think I've died and gone to heaven," Butch beamed.

"And here," Lucas continued, "this is important. Jay

Gould, April 1873 and again in November of that year. Everybody know who Jay Gould was?"

The others nodded. "I don't," I said.

That seemed to please the old lawyer. "Then I'll tell you, son. But first, I'll have to give you a little history of our town. Quincy was settled way back in 1836. Bet Job's Crossing isn't that old, eh, son?"

"I don't know," I admitted.

"Older," Biggie said.

Lucas looked disappointed, but continued. "At that time, the site was a river landing on Big Cypress Bayou."

"Ain't, uh, isn't it still?"

"I'm getting to that. First things first, son. Well, sir, back then, steamboats came sailing down the bayou and Caddo Lake to the Red River, then on into the mighty Mississippi. The town grew like willows on a creek bank and became a major river port between all points west and north all the way down to New Orleans. Why, we had an opera house, four saloons, five mercantile stores, two livery stables, three hotels, and the finest Carnegie library west of the Mississippi. At one time, up to fifteen steamboats would be lining the docks right here in little Quincy, Texas, taking people and goods up and down the river."

"Hard to believe," Norman Thripp said, his eyes wandering out the window to look at the quiet street.

"God's own truth," the lawyer said, his eyes taking on a faraway look. You would of thought he could actually see the busy dock with workers scurrying around loading and unloading the big paddleboats while ladies with parasols strolled along the decks. "By 1872, over two hundred steamboats a year were landing here, and the population

26

had swelled to thirty thousand people." He looked at me. "That was a right large town in those days, son. We were giving even Galveston a run for its money."

"Uh-huh," I said. "Well, what happened to it?"

"That's where old Jay Gould comes in. You see, son, he was what they used to call a robber baron. He owned a railroad, and he wanted to run it through Quincy because it was such an important place, but he had to get permission from the town council. The town council met and asked themselves why they'd want a noisy, smelly railroad coming through when the town was doing just fine the way it was." He slapped the table. "So they turned him down flat."

"I'll bet he was pretty mad," Butch said.

"Mad? That feller was so livid he put a curse on the town. He said that within a year, grass would be growing in the streets."

"And did it?" I asked.

"Well, just about. Only it had nothing to do with Jay Gould. You see, up on the Red River there was a logjam that had started years ago and was growing bigger every year. It was beginning to interfere with river traffic, so the Corps of Engineers took on the job of doing something about it." Lucas looked sad. "Well, what they decided to do was to dynamite the jam. It cleared the river all right, but it diverted the water away from the Big Cypress Bayou to the point where the boats couldn't get in to our port any longer. Well, now we were left with no port and no railroad either. Yes, sir, Mr. Jay Gould was right about the town. Now, we're just a sleepy little town on the creek—but a proud one with a proud heritage."

Lucas Fitzgerald stopped talking, and everybody was quiet for a long time. Finally, I asked, "Is he the ghost they talk about in the brochure? Jay Gould?"

Alice LaRue let out a snort of laughter. "Shoot, no, son. That's a whole 'nother story. You should get Mary Ann to tell you that one. She knows it well enough. Let's go, folks. It's getting late. We'll have to postpone the rest of our tour." She grabbed her cane and stood up. "Meeting starts here in the morning at nine sharp." She hobbled toward the door leaning on her cane.

"Well," Biggie said. "Let's all go to our rooms and have a little rest before supper."

3

I followed along as Mary Ann led us down a bunch of hallways to our rooms. We twisted and turned, and once or twice I could have sworn we went back the way we'd come, up one short flight of stairs, then down another. The halls were kind of dark, and the doors that lined the walls were painted brown. Finally, we stopped in front of a door with a brass plaque on it that read: OSCAR WILDE ROOM.

"This is your room, Butch," Miss Mary Ann said, taking a key out of her pocket and unlocking the door, then stepping aside for Butch to enter first.

He crossed his hands over his chest and looked around the room, which was decorated in purple and gold. The canopy bed was painted gold and had a spread made of purple velvet. The drapes on the windows matched the spread and there was a gold full-length mirror hanging next to the washstand, which held a white bowl and pitcher edged in gold and decorated with purple violets.

"I just love it!" Butch breathed. "Miss Mary Ann, could it be possible that Oscar Wilde is the ghost of the Imperial Hotel? That would be just *so* cool!"

Miss Mary Ann went over and threw open a window. "I believe Annabeth must have forgotten to air your room out. No, Butch, I'm sorry, but Oscar Wilde hasn't been seen around here for the last hundred years."

"Oh, well," Butch said, touching the soft velvet spread. "His spirit's here. I can just feel it." He walked over and stood before the mirror, then turned sideways and sucked in his stomach as he looked at himself. "Y'all can go on now," he said. "I'll see you at supper."

"Don't mind Butch," Miss Mattie said to Mary Ann as we continued down the hall. "He's a little strange, but he has a heart of gold."

"I think he's charming," Miss Mary Ann said as she turned the key in a door marked LADY BIRD JOHNSON ROOM. "This is the room we selected for the Thripps." She stepped aside to let Miss Mattie enter the room, which was light and airy. The two tall windows had lace curtains and the pale blue walls were covered with pictures of Texas wildflowers.

"Did she . . ." Miss Mattie said.

"No, I'm afraid our beloved former first lady never stayed here at the Imperial, but we set up this room as a tribute to her work in preserving the beauty of the roadways of our state. You know, she is responsible for so many of the wildflowers we enjoy on our Texas roadways in the spring. She was raised not far from here, as you may have heard."

"I know," Miss Mattie said, fingering the silver hand mirror on the marble-topped dresser. The room's just beautiful. I was so afraid our room would be dark and heavy like that awful Oscar Wilde Room. No offense, it's just that I like . . ."

"None taken," Miss Mary Ann said. "We try to offer something for everyone."

As she led us down the hall, around a corner and up a small flight of stairs to Biggie's room, she kept telling us stuff about the hotel.

"The hotel had fallen into wrack and ruin in the fifties before the historical society took it over and renovated it," she said. "You could see sunlight through the holes in the ceiling, and a family of possums had raised several generations of young in the lobby. It was a mess, believe you me!"

"I can imagine," Biggie said. "How did you get the money for the project? It must have cost a mint."

"Goodness, me, that was a problem," Miss Mary Ann said. "Of course, that was before I got into it, but they say the ladies held auctions, bake sales, charity balls, anything they could think of to raise the money. Then they shamelessly prevailed upon any childless widow with an antique to her name to will her things to the project. You'd be surprised how many fine furnishings we obtained by bequest." She gave a little giggle. "And you'd be surprised how many indignant relatives came out of the woodwork to try and break the wills, usually folks who had made themselves plenty scarce during the poor woman's last days." Miss Mary Ann stopped and pointed to a door just to our right. "This is the Jay Gould Room. It is Lucas Fitzgerald's permanent home. And, Biggie, here's your room." She inserted another key and swung open the door.

Biggie's was a corner room with four windows, with white ruffled curtains. The pale green wallpaper was decorated with little pink roses on white trellises. The bed had a pink spread and was piled high with lacy white and pale green pillows.

"This is the finest room in the hotel," Miss Mary Jane said, "the Diamond Lucy Room."

"It's pretty," Biggie said. "Hmm, Diamond Lucy. Where have I heard that?"

Miss Mary Ann winked at me. "Diamond Lucy is our resident ghost. Hers is a fascinating story, which I'll be glad to tell you after supper, if you wish."

"And she stayed in this room?" Biggie asked.

"Well, no, actually." Mary Ann flicked a speck of dust off the dresser with her hankie. "She stayed in one of the rooms down the hall, but the society decided to name our finest room after our most colorful, if not most famous, guest."

I nodded. "Where's my room?"

"You're sharing with Rosebud," Biggie said. She went over and sat down at the dressing table and began taking pins out of her hair. "I'm going to have a little nap. Will you be okay until suppertime?"

"Sure, Biggie." I was already heading out the door. "I'm not a baby, you know."

Me and Rosebud were staying in the Rutherford B. Hayes Room. It was all done in emerald green with heavy, dark furniture. Mary Ann opened a door next to the bed and said, "This is your private bath. Normally, you'd have to share it with the room next door, but that room is never used, so you'll have it all to yourself."

I was hardly listening as I went back to the bedroom. On the marble-topped washstand, I had spotted a big-screen TV with a pile of video games stacked next to it. On the opposite side of the TV sat a little scented votive candle and an ashtray with a book of matches marked IMPER-IAL HOTEL.

"I don't smoke," I said.

Miss Mary Ann laughed. "That's okay. Maybe you'll use the ashtray to put gum wrappers in."

"Will you be okay until Rosebud gets back?" Miss Mary Ann asked as she turned to go.

"Yes, ma'am!" I was already checking out the video games.

"Supper's at six-thirty," she said with a smile, closing the door behind her.

I played games for an hour, then turned on the TV and watched talk shows for a while. Biggie doesn't like me watching those shows, but I feel you can learn a lot from them. For instance, I know for a fact that I will never *ever* have affairs with members of my family or get into fist-fights with members of the opposite sex. Also, if I ever decide to get a tattoo, it will not be a picture of a hula dancer or a bloody dagger.

When I came down for supper an hour later, Rosebud and Mr. Thripp were sitting at a small table in the lobby playing chess. I stood watching for a few minutes but nobody seemed to notice me.

"Did you get the car fixed?" I asked.

Both of them ignored me. Mr. Thripp frowned at the board and kept putting his hand on one of his men, then moving it to another. Rosebud sat with his chin in his hand, a little smile crinkling the corner of his mouth. Finally, Mr. Thripp moved one of his pawns and Rosebud, quick as a flash, made his move and toppled Mr. Thripp's king.

"Say what?" Rosebud finally looked at me.

"Did you get the car fixed?" I said again.

"Wasn't nothing wrong with it," he said with a wink. "Me and Norman here, we just wasn't all that interested in touring the hotel, so we found us a nice little ice cream parlor down the street and had ourselves a banana split."

Just as I was about to tell him thanks a lot for not taking me along, a little gong rang from somewhere in the back of the hotel, and Miss Mary Ann came into the lobby. Biggie, Miss Mattie, and Butch came down the stairs together followed by Lucas Fitzgerald.

"Supper is ready in the courtyard," Mary Ann said.

We followed her down the hall past a small room with a few tables and chairs and a bar across one wall. Miss Mary Ann said that was the lounge, and it was only opened when guests requested it. A little farther on, we came to a pair of French doors that led to an open area in the middle of the building. Ivy climbed up the white-painted brick walls and clung to the upper balcony, which had a wrought-iron railing stretched across it. I could see tall windows behind the railing. A thick hedge of azalea bushes hid the foundation of the building and dripped white and pink blossoms all along the pathway. Hanging baskets filled with bougainvillea bloomed everywhere, and in one corner the biggest crepe myrtle I'd ever seen grew all the way up to the balcony. Miss Mary Ann saw me looking at it.

"That tree's over a hundred years old," she said. "Isn't it something?"

Biggie walked over and touched its smooth bark. "This old tree must have seen a lot," she said.

"I expect so," Miss Mary Ann said and swept her arm toward the table. "Please have a seat. Annabeth will be serving the food as soon as you're all seated."

The table, spread with a pink cloth, was set next to a stone fountain in the middle of the courtyard. In the middle of the fountain stood a bronze statue of a young woman wearing nothing but a drape. She was holding a pitcher. Water ran from the pitcher and splashed onto the goldfish swimming in the round pond beneath her feet. Lily pads floated on top of the water.

Butch walked over and stood in front of the statue. "That is just so beautiful," he said. "Reminds me of New Orleans. Mattie, you and Norman ought to do something like this out behind the tearoom. I could design you something real nice."

"Oh, yes," Miss Mattie said. "We could serve lunch out there when the weather is nice."

Mr. Thripp shook his head. "There's nothing but an alley behind our building," he said. "Where would you put the Dumpster?"

"Let's all take a seat," Biggie said. "Dinner's getting cold."

Biggie took her place at the head of the table and Miss

Mary Ann sat at the other end. Me, Rosebud, the Tripps, and the lawyer found places on either side of them. There were still two empty spaces at the table. Miss Mary Ann rang a little glass bell beside her plate and instantly Annabeth came through the door followed by Brian, who was carrying a large tray. Brian helped Annabeth as she served each of us a bowl of cold, green soup, then they sat down at the two extra places.

I tasted mine. "Uck!" I said. Biggie gave me a look, and I knew better than to say more, but I'll tell you the truth, I thought it tasted exactly like pond scum. Miss Mary Ann said it was cucumber-dill soup. After the soup, Brian and Annabeth cleared away the soup plates and brought in individual chicken pot pies. I have to admit, they were almost as good as Willie Mae's. The crust was buttery and crisp, the inside filled with chunks of white chicken and little baby peas and onions swimming in creamy gravy. For dessert, we had fresh strawberries served on crispy biscuits with whipped cream on top.

Mr. Thripp tilted back in his chair and patted his little round tummy. "Right good," he said. "Mattie, we ought to get the recipe for that pot pie for the tearoom."

"Sit up straight, Norman," Miss Mattie said. "You're about to break that chair."

Sure enough, just as she said that, I heard a cracking noise and the little back legs of the chair gave way, dumping Mr. Thripp on the ground in a jumble of skinny arms and legs.

"My soul, Norman. Look what you've gone and done." Miss Mattie could have been a little more sympathetic, if you ask me.

"Ooow," Mr. Thripp said.

Rosebud jumped up and, taking him under his arms, lifted him to his feet. "Can you stand up?"

Mr. Thripp took one step. "I guess so," he said, "but I believe I'll just go sit on the sofa for awhile." He hobbled toward the door.

Biggie and Miss Mattie, busy examining the damage to the antique chair, didn't look up.

"I'll have Annabeth serve the coffee in the lobby parlor," Miss Mary Ann said. "Ladies, don't worry about the chair. We have an excellent furniture restorer here in town. I'm sure he can fix it good as new."

"Good as old," I said.

Everybody looked at me until I turned red. Then Miss Mary Ann herded us all into the lobby. After the coffee was served, Annabeth and Brian went upstairs to get ready for the dance. When they came back down, Annabeth was wearing a white dress with lace at the sleeves and hem. Her hair was pulled back from her face, and she wore a white gardenia behind her ear.

"You are a vision of loveliness," Lucas Fitzgerald said. I agreed. She looked like pictures I'd seen of Greek goddesses.

"You promised to tell us about the ghost," I said after they left.

"So I did." Mary Ann patted her knees and beamed at me. "Everybody want to hear?" When they all nodded, she commenced. "This is the story of one Maudie Morgan, also known as Diamond Lucy. She was born in Kansas City, Missouri, the daughter of a livery stable owner and his wife in the late 1850s. It was said she grew to be the most beautiful girl in town with long golden curls and skin the color of cream. All the boys in town wanted to marry her, but she snubbed them all. You see, she had dreams of becoming an actress on the stage. One day, she met up with a drummer and ran away with him, hoping to find fame and fortune in New York City."

"Silly girl," Mr. Thripp muttered.

"Shut up, Norman," Miss Mattie said.

"You mean he played the drums?" I asked.

"No, dear," Miss Mary Ann said. "A drummer is an old-timey word for a traveling salesman. Sadly, the poor girl never made it to New York. Within a year, she had fallen in with the wrong crowd and soon found herself working in a brothel in Hot Springs, Arkansas."

"What's . . ."

"I'll tell you later," Biggie said. "Now, hush and let Mary Ann tell her story.

"Apparently, she was good at her work," Mary Ann continued, "because soon she was bedecked with diamonds—rubies and emeralds and pearls, too, so they say. That's how she got the name of Diamond Lucy."

Lucas Fitzgerald held out his coffee cup, and Mary Ann filled it from the silver pot on the table in front of her.

"Fascinating," Biggie said. "So, how did it happen that she came to Quincy?"

"We don't exactly know," Mary Ann said. "What we do know is, she met a man named Sol Reingold who had an affinity for liquor, gambling, and prostitutes. They were married in Arkansas and came to Quincy around 1877. The arrived on a steamboat and registered right here at the Imperial Hotel. The town was all abuzz with talk about the new couple because they were a fine-looking pair, always dressed in the latest fashions from New York and Paris. Lucy always wore her diamonds, day and night, even in the morning when she browsed through the shops along Main Street while Sol passed his time entertaining the men in the barbershop with stories of his adventures in faraway places. Behind her back, the ladies accused Lucy of being flashy, but the truth was, they were green with envy and competed with each other to be the first to invite the handsome pair to their dinner parties and soirees."

"Folks just don't change," Miss Mattie commented.

"They called themselves Mr. and Mrs. Woodrow Hamilton, and readily accepted most invitations." Mary Ann twisted the little wedding band on her finger. "The men played poker while the women took tea in the parlor." She smiled. "Often, the men found their wallets a good bit lighter at the end of those evenings."

"Huh?" I said.

"He won their money," Biggie said. "Now hush and listen."

Mr. Thripp stood up. "Think I'll turn in," he said. No one paid him any attention, so he hobbled on up the stairs.

Mary Ann continued. "Soon, the couple let it be known that they were expecting a child. Months went by and, though large with child, Lucy continued to be seen around town wearing her fine clothes and jewelry."

"Reminds me of Clarice Mayfield," Miss Mattie said. "Remember, Biggie? We thought she was going to have her baby on the courthouse steps."

"That woman loved to shop," Butch said. "I heard she ordered all her maternity clothes from Neiman Marcus."

"The baby was born with a great big head," Miss Mattie said. "Oh, there was nothing wrong with it. All the Mayfields had big heads . . . but Clarice vowed after that one, she'd never have another baby."

"They moved to Gladewater. He went into the beer business," Butch said.

Biggie slapped the arm of her chair. "Will you two hush and let Mary Ann get on with her story?"

They hushed and Miss Mary Ann continued.

"You know how, in the middle of winter, we get a little warm spell? Well, it was one of those warm days in January that Mr. Hamilton stopped by Henrique's restaurant and purchased a picnic lunch. He told the waiter they thought they'd just take advantage of the nice weather. They were last seen together crossing the bridge across the bayou toward Brinker's Woods carrying a picnic basket. She was smiling up at him and he had his arm around her waist. Late that evening, he returned alone." She paused and looked at us.

"Wow," I said. "Did he kill her?"

"No one knew at first." Mary Ann took a sip of her coffee. "Sol said she had stayed to visit friends on the other side of the bayou, but he left on the next boat bound for New Orleans. He was carrying all of Lucy's carpetbags and hatboxes. Strange, the people thought. Lucy was never seen alive again."

"Did they find her?" Biggie asked.

"Well, eventually. You see, after that one little warm spell, the worst winter anyone could remember followed.

It snowed and sleeted through the entire month of February. One day, toward the end of the month, one Seth Milliken, a farmer, discovered her body beside the road. It was perfectly preserved because of the freezing weather. The snow around her was covered with blood. People concluded that she must had given birth to her baby out there and the poor thing was carried away by the wild hogs that roam those woods to this day."

"Yuck," I said.

"The story persists to this day that a trapper found the baby alive and took it home to raise." Lucas held out his coffee cup for Mary Ann to refill. "Who knows, Diamond Lucy's descendants may dwell nearby, even today."

"Now, Lucas, that's just an old rumor. A newborn baby couldn't have survived for five minutes in that cold." Miss Mary Ann poured his coffee and offered him the sugar bowl.

"Who knows?" Lucas said, looking wise. "Anyway, they brought her body back to town, and she lay in state right here in this lobby for a day. After all, this had been her only home in Quincy. The townspeople took up a collection to give her a decent burial. They purchased a nice stone and built a little iron fence to go around her grave."

"Fresh flowers appear at her graveside every year on the date she was last seen alive—daffodils and tulips," Miss Mary Ann said.

"What a sad story." Biggie shook her head.

"At least she was laid away right," Miss Mattie said.

"You'd think so," Mary Ann said, "but she never has gone to her rest. She still walks the halls of this hotel, and some nights, her moans and tears are just heartrending."

I felt a chill just thinking about it. "Where does she stay most?" I asked, hoping it wasn't near my room.

"She seems to like the courtyard best," Mary Ann answered. "The bronze statue in the fountain was paid for by a secret admirer two years after her death. Some say the face of the statue is identical to Lucy's."

"Aren't there any pictures of her?" I asked.

"No photographs," she said, "but there is a tintype in the museum. It's blurred with age, so you can't really tell much about her. If you ask, I'm sure Lucas will show it to you tomorrow."

Lucas nodded.

Up until now, Rosebud had been quiet, just sipping his coffee and listening to the story. Now he spoke up. "What happened to her husband?"

"He was found in a New Orleans brothel, a mere skeleton from drink and disease. He had tried to kill himself but only succeeded in shooting out his left eye. He lived to stand trial here in Quincy and was sentenced to death. A hanging was scheduled but, at the last minute, a judge overturned the verdict, saying he had not gotten a fair trial. He disappeared after that and was never heard from again."

Biggie looked at her watch. "My soul, it's almost eleven. I'm going to bed."

I followed Biggie up the stairs, wondering if I'd ever get one wink of sleep in this haunted hotel.

4

The halls of the hotel, papered in faded wallpaper and lit by hanging sconces with little flame bulbs, looked spooky in the semidarkness. My shadow along the walls looked like a skinny old witch, and the walls and floor seemed to creak and moan with each step I took. When I finally got to my room, I turned on all the lights before going into the bathroom to brush my teeth. Suddenly, the door to the room next door made me uncomfortable. I locked the dead bolt on my side. Then I took off my clothes and crawled into bed taking the TV remote with me. I turned on *World's Scariest Cop Chases* but it was one I'd already seen. I watched it awhile, then started getting sleepy. I dozed off with the television on and never even heard Rosebud when he came up to bed.

It must have been after midnight when I woke up with a dry throat. I was dying for a drink of water but I was too sleepy to get up. I turned over in bed and tried to get back to sleep, but it was no good. I had to have a drink. I pushed back the covers and crawled out of the bed. Rosebud must have opened the drapes before he came to bed, because the moonlight was streaming in through the windows. I could see the shapes of the branches from the old crepe myrtle swaying in the wind. I went into the bathroom, turned on the light, and looked for a drinking glass beside the sink, but there was not one. I'd have to ask Miss Mary Ann for one tomorrow. In the meantime, I turned on the water and pushed my face under the faucet to drink. The water came out brownish-looking and tasted like iron, but I was too thirsty to care. As I turned off the water and was wiping my face with a towel, I heard a sound coming from the next room, real soft at first, then it got louder. It sounded like a baby kitten mewing for its mama. I stood still and listened. Now, it came again, only fainter. Finally, it stopped completely. I went back to the bed and crawled under the covers, but the moon was shining in my face, so I got up and closed the drapes. Just as I was dozing off again, Rosebud gave a big snort in his sleep, and I like to jumped out of my skin. This haunted hotel must be getting to me, I thought, and scooted as far away from him as I could.

It must have been an hour later that I heard the sound again, this time loud enough to break into a dream I was having. I got out of bed and started back to the bathroom, but now it was dark, since I had closed the drapes. I tripped over one of Rosebud's big shoes and looked at Rosebud, half hoping I had waked him up, but he only turned over in bed and snorted in his sleep. I tiptoed to the window and opened the drapes so I could see my way, then went into the bathroom, and switched on the light. There was no doubt, the sound was coming from the vacant room next door, and it sure wasn't any kitten; it was a woman crying, crying her eyes out. It seemed to me like the sobs were just going to tear her right in two. I turned to go get Rosebud, but then I heard another voice, a man's voice, and it didn't sound like any ghost. I put my ear next to the door, but the voices had stopped. I don't know what got into my head, because I'm not usually very brave, but for some reason, I decided to do a little investigating on my own. I would have called Rosebud, but he sometimes tends to get grumpy when you wake him up unless you've got a very good reason.

I unlocked the door from my side and gave the doorknob a turn, pushing as I did. I was surprised that it swung open so easily. The room was dark as pitch and quiet as a tomb.

"Uh, hello," I whispered. "Anybody in here?"

No one answered, but I had a funny feeling, like I was not alone in that room. It felt like a kind of electricity. The hair on my arms raised up the way it does when you comb your hair and then hold the comb just over your arm. I took one step into the room and stared into the darkness. Pretty soon my eyes adjusted so I could see the shape of an old-timey canopy bed and a tall wardrobe against the wall where I thought the hall door must be. I took another step and stopped again to listen. Could I hear breathing? I couldn't tell, so I whispered again, "Anybody here?"

Just then, I felt an icy breeze whisper past me and move on off toward the door that led to the hall. When I looked, I thought I saw a dim light at the door, then it was gone. The door never opened, but suddenly I knew I was alone in the room.

I ran back to my own room and shook Rosebud. "Wake up! Rosebud, wake up. I just saw the ghost!"

"Say what?" Rosebud rubbed his eyes and looked at me.

"I saw—well, I didn't exactly see her—I felt her. The ghost, Rosebud. Get up. We've got to go find her."

"How come we've got to find her?" Rosebud sat up in bed. "And how come you to be so sure it's a her, anyway?"

"Because, it's Diamond Lucy." I gave Rosebud a shove. "Get up. Come on." I jumped down and fished my shoes out from under the bed.

Rosebud wouldn't budge until I told him everything from the woman's sobs to the cold way she brushed past me and disappeared without having to open the door. "If you won't come with me, I'm going by myself." I was already pulling on my jeans over my pajamas. "This may be the last chance I ever have to see a real live ghost!"

Rosebud slung his long black legs over the side of the bed. "Hand me my pants," he said.

I stood on one foot and then the other while Rosebud put on his pants over the tee shirt he was wearing and took forever getting into his socks and shoes.

When he was finally done, I led him into the room next door. Rosebud stopped in the middle of the room and sniffed the air, wrinkling his nose.

"Smell that?" he asked.

"What?" I sniffed the air. "Oh, yeah." It smelled like

the ground does when you crawl real far under Biggie's house—like rotten leaves and earthworms and old damp bricks.

"Come on." He left the room and went back to our room, opening the door to the hall. Everything looked normal, just like it had when I came up to bed. The sconces with candle flame bulbs still shone dimly against the faded wallpaper. Somewhere in the hotel, I heard somebody snoring. Probably Biggie, who snores like a freight train, but just try to get her to admit it. I waited for Rosebud to say I was being silly and let's go back to bed. Instead, he started down the hall toward the stairs. I followed. When we came to the lobby, he made a beeline for the big desk and began rummaging around in the drawers like he owned the place.

"Rosebud, you might not oughta be doing that," I whispered. "What if someone catches you?"

Rosebud ignored me and went right on prowling through drawers and shelves. Finally he pulled a flashlight out from Miss Mary Ann's sewing basket. He turned it on to test it, and motioned for me to follow him down the long hall that led to the back of the hotel.

"Where are we going, Rosebud?" I had to run to keep up with his long strides.

Rosebud didn't answer, just kept walking until he came to the French doors to the courtyard. He switched off the flashlight on account of the moon was almost as bright as day. Rosebud didn't open the door, just peered through the glass panes. I cupped my hands around my eyes and looked too. That courtyard looked pretty in the moonlight. Shadows from the trees and vines danced on the brick floor and the bright reflections in the water from the fountain made the statue gleam like silver.

"Let's go on back now. There's nothing here." Everything looked so normal, I had decided I must have been dreaming after all.

Just then, Rosebud pointed. Something was moving across the bricks. It was light, but it wasn't light, and it cast a shadow. It disappeared into the shadows under the old crepe myrtle tree. The thing reminded me of the foxfire I'd seen in the woods one night when Rosebud had taken me and Monica camping. Monica had insisted it was "haunts" but Rosebud explained to us that it was only phosphorous that was coming out of the swampy ground. Then we heard a low moan, both fearful and sad, followed by a loud thump. I gripped Rosebud's arm. The sounds seemed to come from somewhere under our feet. We waited a few minutes more, but nothing happened. Finally, Rosebud opened the doors and stepped out into the courtyard, shining his flashlight in all the nooks and crannies. "It's gone," he said and turned back toward the stairs.

"Rosebud," I said after he had closed the drapes and crawled back in bed, "where do you reckon those sounds came from?"

"I dunno," he said. "Go to sleep."

I had one other question I just had to ask. "Rosebud, do you really believe in ghosts?"

"Yep." He turned over on his side and wouldn't say another word.

The next morning I woke up and looked at the old carved clock on the wall. Only six o'clock, but the sun was already making bright slices between the heavy drapes. I went over and peeped between the folds, making sure not to let in enough light to wake Rosebud. I was surprised to find that the windows weren't windows at all, but French doors—and they led to the balcony that surrounded the courtyard. I turned the handle on the door, but it was locked. Then I noticed a bolt just under the handle. When I turned that, the door opened and swung out without making a sound. As I stepped out into the muggy East Texas morning, I heard somebody banging garbage cans down the street. Two cardinals made a racket as they argued over the seeds on the crepe myrtle tree. A yellow cat was licking itself on one of the iron benches. Everything looked so normal I was convinced I had imagined the whole thing last night. Then my eyes fell on the fountain. I screamed. I screamed and screamed until Rosebud came bursting out the door and grabbed me in his arms.

5

Later, downstairs in the lobby, I sat shivering on a velvet-covered bench with Rosebud's arm still around me. Butch sat on the other side patting me on the hand. Brian, with tears in his eyes, sat on one of the sofas next to his mother, who was smoothing his hair and whispering to him. The undertaker had already come and taken Annabeth away. He had wheeled the stretcher through the lobby, her body covered with a white sheet. Now, we were all gathered together to wait for the sheriff to come and start trying to find out why someone had left Annabeth lying faceup in the fountain with a butcher knife sticking out of her chest. I closed my eyes and tried to wipe away the sight of her dead eyes staring up at me through the cloudy water. Mostly, I tried to forget how the goldfish were all gathered around fighting over who was going to get to gobble up the blood that was oozing out of her wound. I never wanted to see another goldfish as long as I lived. I didn't care how pretty they were.

Biggie, who had been walking around questioning everybody, came over and hugged me. "Rosebud, why don't you take J.R. out for an ice-cream cone while we wait?"

"I wouldn't care for any ice cream right now," I said, trying to sound like a grown-up, because I sure didn't feel like one. A strange man was sitting at the game table talking to Mr. Thripp. "Who's that?" I asked.

Biggie glanced at the tall man, who wore a black suit. He was staring at Miss Mary Ann. While I was watching, he got up and took a step toward her, then changed his mind and sat back down. "His name's Lew Masters. He says he's a casket salesman from Shreveport. He checked in late last night after we all went upstairs."

Just then, there was a commotion at the front door as the members of the historical society came into the lobby together. Hen Lester carried a manila folder in her hands. She tapped Alice LaRue on the shoulder, and they both stopped and looked at some papers in the folder. Alice nodded, then Hen closed the folder and they both approached Biggie. Emily Faye followed behind, glancing at Brian like she could eat him with a spoon.

"Here we are," Alice said, "all fired up to teach you all we know about local history. Hey, why's everybody look like they just had a dose of castor oil, anyway? It's not going to be all that bad!"

At that very moment, Lucas Fitzgerald came down the stairs from his room, looking at his gold pocket watch and frowning. "You're five minutes late," he scolded.

Biggie told them what had happened.

"Oh, I think I'm going to faint." Hen Lester grabbed the arm of the chair in front of her.

"Don't you dare faint, Hen." Alice LaRue took her by the arm and shoved her down on the sofa. "Put your head between your legs."

Mary Ann nodded and watched the door as two men dressed in khaki and wearing badges came into the lobby. They both had pistols in black holsters attached to their belts. One was tall and shaped like a gorilla. He had broad shoulders, tiny hips, and arms that reached almost to his knees, and when he walked his head and shoulders got there before the rest of him. He had hair growing out of his ears. The other was the spitting image of Barney Fife from the old *Andy Griffith Show*.

The big man went straight to Miss Mary Ann and leaned over to talk to her. After a few minutes, he straightened up and faced the rest of us. "Folks, why don't you all take a seat, and we'll see if we can get to the bottom of this. Miz Lester, you reckon you could scoot over and let Miss Alice and Emily sit between you and Lawyer Fitzgerald? That's good." He looked at the rest of us. "Let's see, now. I don't believe I've met all you folks. Why don't we just take turns and introduce ourselves so as I can see where I'm going here." He moved to the center of the circle while the other man sat in a straight chair and took a tape recorder out of a bag he had been carrying. He turned it on and balanced it on his knees. "Now then." The sheriff took a pair of old-timey wire-rim glasses out of his pocket and put them on. "I'm Sheriff Roswell Dugger, and this here's my deputy, Elmore Wiggs. Now then, when I point to you, go ahead and state your name and where you're from. You, sir?" He looked at Mr. Thripp.

"I'm Norman Thripp from over in Job's Crossing, and this is my wife, Mathilda. We never saw this young woman before in our lives. We're just here for . . ."

The sheriff interrupted him. "What say we just get names and addresses first? I'll ask questions later." Mr. Thripp gave his address and the sheriff turned to Butch, who I was glad to see was wearing plain jeans and a tee shirt that said GOD BLESS JOHN WAYNE on the front. I hoped the sheriff didn't notice the daisies printed on his sox.

Butch crossed one leg over the other and put his hands on his knees. He spoke in a deep voice I hardly recognized as Butch. "Theodore P. Hickley, 204 Pecan Street, Job's Crossing, Texas."

Rosebud put his hand to his mouth, but not before I saw the smile he was trying to hide. The sheriff skipped over Rosebud and looked at Biggie, who sat up as tall as she could considering that she's only four foot eleven, and answered, "Fiona Wooten Weatherford, 206 Elm Street, Job's Crossing, Texas."

"Weatherford," the sheriff said. "Seems to me like I've heard that name before—connected to Job's Crossing, too."

"She's always solving murders," I piped up. Rosebud pinched me. "Ow!"

"They call you Biggie?"

"Yes," Biggie said.

"Well, ma'am. I have heard about you, and I'd be mighty grateful if you'd just let us handle this here little matter."

Biggie smiled her sweetest smile. "Why, of course, Sheriff. I wouldn't think of interfering in your investigation. My goodness, we're just here to study the methods of your excellent historical society."

The sheriff nodded and began questioning each person in the room starting with Brian.

I was glad that the doctor, who had come earlier to examine Annabeth's body, had given him a sedative to calm him down. I could still hear his screams when they told him about the murder. Brian's voice was flat as he told the sheriff about how he and Annabeth had come home from the dance around one o'clock. He had been hungry, so they had gone into the kitchen and raided the icebox, making cold chicken sandwiches and drinking tea. After they finished, he walked Annabeth to her room and then went to his own room and went to sleep. "I conked out right away," he said, his voice breaking. "I wish I hadn't drunk so much beer at the dance—I might have heard something." He put his head down and started sobbing like a baby.

The sheriff turned to Miss Mary Ann. "How about you, ma'am?"

Miss Mary Ann looked at Brian with tears in her eyes. She shook herself and turned to the sheriff. "Oh, lordy, I don't know if I can remember. Everything's happened so fast." She dabbed at her eyes with the Kleenex she was holding. "It's all just so terrible. Let me think a minute. Um . . . well, Annabeth and Brian helped me with the dinner dishes for a little while, but I could see they were wanting to get out to the dance, so I sent them on off. After

I finished the kitchen, I went into my room to watch my shows on TV." She got up and went over to where Brian was sitting. She put her hand on his shoulder, but he shook her off.

"Which room is yours?" The sheriff held up his hand. "Hold it a minute. Looks like Wiggs here's run out of tape." While the deputy replaced the tape in his recorder, the sheriff walked over to the coffee urn on the desk and filled a mug with coffee, and when he did, I noticed that he was holding his side like it hurt. "Anybody else?" His face was pale as he turned to face the room. Everybody shook their heads.

After the deputy had the tape running again, Miss Mary Ann continued. "It's a suite, really, a bedroom and a little sitting room. It's that door there." She pointed to a door just past the bar. "It's the only sleeping quarters on the first floor. All the guest rooms are upstairs."

"So, you're watching TV in your room. Hear anything?"

"Well, yes. You see, just as *Eyewitness News* out of Shreveport was starting, the bell on the door tinkled, and I went out to the lobby to see who had come in. It was Mr. Masters, here." She pointed to the man in the suit. "He was supposed to check in before six, but he had car trouble."

Mr. Lew Masters nodded. "That's right, Sheriff. It was just shortly after ten. I was tired, so I went right up to my room and went to bed."

"Did you know the young lady, the deceased?"

"Well, yes." Mr. Masters got up to pour himself a mug

of coffee, and returned to his place by the table. "You see, this hotel is on my regular route. I try to call on all the funeral directors in the northeast Texas area at least twice a year, and I make it a point to be in Quincy by nightfall because Miss Mary Ann takes such good care of me." He smiled at Miss Mary Ann, who blushed.

"Well," the sheriff said, looking at the historical society members, "I assume you folks don't know much, seeing as how you got here just before we did. Does anyone have anything to add? Anything you might know about the deceased?"

Brian spoke up. "Her name is Annabeth. Stop calling her the deceased!"

The sheriff ignored him. "Well?"

"She's part of that Baugh family that lives out on the lake." Hen Lester looked like she smelled something nasty.

"She was absolutely beautiful," Alice LaRue said, "and a nice girl. Shame on you, Hen."

Lucas Fitzgerald nodded, but didn't say anything. Emily LaRue stared out the window.

The sheriff turned to me, rubbing his hands together. "Wellsir, I reckon it's time to question our little star player. I understand you saw her first, sonny."

"Yes, sir."

"Well, what can you tell me?"

"She was in the fountain. The fishes were eating her blood." I felt the sweet roll I'd eaten for breakfast coming back up. I swallowed hard and continued. "That's all I know."

"Hear anything during the night?"

I told him I thought I'd heard something in the next room.

The sheriff nodded and turned to Rosebud. "How 'bout you?"

Rosebud told the sheriff about how I'd woke him up and how we'd come downstairs and borrowed a flashlight to look around.

"They wasn't nothing to see," Rosebud said. "Courtyard was empty. We looked around a little bit then came on back up and went to bed."

"And that was what time?"

Rosebud looked at me. "Twelve-thirty," I said.

"Go on," the sheriff said.

"That's about it," Rosebud said. "Around six, I heard my boy screamin' like the hounds of hell were after him."

The sheriff nodded and motioned the deputy to turn off his recorder. "Okay, that about does it. I'm taping off the courtyard as a crime scene and, until we finish with the investigation, I'll have to ask you all to stay out of there— and not to leave town."

"For how long?" Lew Masters asked. "I've got my calls to make."

"No more than a few days, I expect. I don't reckon your clients are going anywhere." The sheriff chuckled at his own joke and started for the door, then turned and faced the room. "You folks just go on about your business. Try and forget about this murder." He looked at Biggie, who smiled sweetly back at him. "All right, then. I'll be in touch if I have any further questions."

"Sheriff," Biggie said. "Aren't you going to question

each of us separately? It's my understanding that that is the proper procedure."

"Later," the sheriff said. "Right now, I don't feel so hot. Must have been something I ate." He turned and walked out the door, leaning to the right and holding on to his side.

6

After the sheriff left, Miss Mary Ann and Brian got up and went back toward the kitchen. The rest of us stayed in the lobby talking until Miss Mary Ann came and announced lunch was ready. We all trooped into the big dining room. Brian was setting water glasses on one long table in the middle of the room. An antique sideboard stood against the wall and was covered with platters of deli sandwiches, big bowls of chips, and a tray loaded with several kinds of pickles, black and green olives, and jalapeño peppers stuffed with cream cheese. Another tray held soft drinks of every kind you could think of. On a small table nearby, slices of peach, cherry, and apple pie rested on little plates.

Miss Mary Ann, wearing a pink dress with a white ruffled collar, stood in front of the table and held her hands up. "I apologize for the makeshift meal, but I'm lost without Annabeth." She sighed and pushed a silver curl behind her ear. "Never mind, I'll think of something. In the meantime, the people at the Copper Pot deli were kind enough to provide this meal for us."

I saw Biggie whisper something in Rosebud's ear. He nodded.

I helped myself to a tuna salad sandwich on sun-flower-seed bread with chips, black olives, which I can't get enough of, and a large orange soda. Normally, I would have had a Big Red, but I believe seeing all that blood has about killed my appetite for my favorite soda. Maybe I'll get over it. I hope so, because I used to love Big Reds just about better than anything.

Mr. Fitzgerald patted me on the back and hung his cane over the back of his chair before he took a seat at the table. "How are you holding up, youngun?"

"Okay, I guess." I didn't much want to talk about last night, but was pretty sure I was going to have to.

"Bet you were pretty scared. Huh?" Alice, who was sitting next to me, smelled like lawn mower fuel. She popped a chip in her mouth before taking a big bite out of her corned beef on pumpernickel.

"Yes, ma'am."

"Did you hear anything during the night?" Mr. Fitzgerald wasn't going to give up.

"Only the ghost."

I was busy eating my sandwich, so it took a few seconds for me to realize that everyone in the room had stopped talking and were staring at me. "What?" I said.

"J.R., you didn't say anything about any ghost," Biggie said.

"No'm."

Alice picked up her fork, then put it down again. She put her big old elbows on the table and leaned toward me. "Tell me all about it, boy," she said. "The last person to see old Lucy was . . ."

"Abraham Tilley," Lucas put in. "Back in, let me see, nineteen-oh-one, I believe it was."

"Well, now isn't that a coincidence," Hen Lester said from across the table. "Wasn't that the night Maudelle Baugh was killed? And wasn't she helping out in the kitchen, just like this girl was?"

"My soul." Biggie popped a chip in her mouth. "Now, isn't that a coincidence?" She looked around at the shocked expressions on everybody's faces. "Well, surely you don't think there's any connection? Besides, there's no such thing as ghosts."

I breathed a sigh of relief. If Biggie said there were no ghosts, I believed her. Biggie's never wrong. Still, I knew Willie Mae would never lie, and she said she did believe. I felt the lump crawl back into my throat. When it came to the spirit world, I had to go with Willie Mae. After all, she was an expert on those things, being a voodoo lady and all.

"How did Maudelle Baugh get killed?" Butch squirmed around in his chair to face Lucas.

Miss Mary Ann had been sitting at the end of the table with Lew Masters. Suddenly, she stood up and faced the room. "She was shot in the back with a Colt .45," she said. "They never found who did it. Anybody want coffee?" Several of the adults nodded, so she got up and served coffee all around.

"You're wrong," Lucas said. "Her husband did it.

Maudelle was going to leave him for a railroad man. My papa used to tell about the incident. It happened shortly before I came into this world."

"Are you sure that was Abraham Tilley?" Hen Lester asked. "I thought he was the abolitionist."

"The abolitionist was Hosiah Tilley." Alice drained her Diet Coke. "He was Abraham's granddaddy, I think. That right, Lucas?"

"You had an abolitionist here in Quincy?" Biggie laid down her sandwich and looked at Alice. "I would have thought a person with those views would have been ridden out of town on a rail."

"Not so." Lucas pulled a cigar out of his pocket and sniffed it. He noticed Hen Lester glaring at him. "Don't worry, Hen. I'm not going to light it," he said and turned back to Biggie. "During the years before the Civil War, we had all kinds of people with divergent views living in this town. Quite cosmopolitan, actually, what with the river travel, and all." He sniffed his cigar and put it in his mouth. "Hosiah Tilley owned this very hotel and the livery stable that used to be next door."

"He helped runaway slaves," Alice LaRue said. "Emily, honey, get me a piece of that apple pie." Emily LaRue jumped up and got the pie off the long table. She set a clean fork and a fresh paper napkin next to it in front of Alice before sitting down and continuing to eat her sandwich. When she ate, she took little, bitty bites, pecking at her food like a chicken.

"How'd he do that?" I asked, interested in spite of myself.

"He would hide them in a secret place here in the hotel

62

until dark, then provide them with a twenty-dollar gold piece, a good horse, and a map." Lucas took a sip of his coffee.

"My lord, how did that help them?" Biggie asked. "Texas was a slave state. They would have been hunted down and brought back."

"Some were," Lucas said, "but the map he gave them was to show them the way to the Indian Territory, which was no more than fifty miles from here. On a good horse, a man could make it there before sunrise. Then he could disappear into the wilderness. Many of the runaway slaves ended up merging with the Indian tribes, others found their way into Missouri or Kansas where some became cowboys, some joined the Union Army."

"Hosiah Tilley was not a gentleman," Hen Lester said.

"He met his wife in a saloon over in Shreveport, is what I heard," Miss Mary Ann put in. "She was common."

"Where in the hotel did he hide the slaves?" Biggie wondered.

"Nobody knows," Lucas said. "The law searched the place over and over again, but never found a single black soul."

"And he never, ever wore a coat and tie, even at his papa's funeral," Hen Lester continued. "And they say his children ran the streets like little savages."

"Still, he was a good man," Alice said, popping a piece of pie in her mouth. "Now, let's let the boy tell us about the ghost."

I told them about hearing sounds in the next room and about how I thought it was someone crying, so I went to check it out.

"Was it a woman—or a child?" Hen Lester wanted to know.

"I don't know, a woman, I guess," I said. "Anyway, when I went in there, I couldn't see anything. Then it went away."

"Well, don't worry, son," Alice said. "Old Lucy's been walking these halls for over a hundred years, and she hasn't hurt anybody yet."

"Idabel and Cloyd Johnson were the social leaders in town back in Lucy's day," Hen Lester said. "They were the first to entertain her and her husband—a costume party, I believe it was . . ."

"No, it was the Hawkeses," Lucas corrected her, "and it was a garden party."

After that, the conversation got really boring. They kept on talking about how it used to be in Quincy—and they told it just like it had happened yesterday. If you ask me, these people were weird. They discussed things that had happened fifty or a hundred years ago as if they were current events. I finished my sandwich, ate a piece of cherry pie, then I asked to be excused. When Biggie nodded, I left the table and went out into the lobby where I found Brian sprawled across one of the sofas holding a copy of *Texas Monthly*, but he wasn't reading it; he was staring into space. I saw a tear roll down his cheek.

He looked so depressed, I thought I'd cheer him up, so I asked if he liked fishing.

"What? Oh, yeah, sort of. I used to anyway."

"Where do you go?"

"Caddo Lake, mostly. They've got catfish as big as an alligator under some of those cypress logs."

"Man! You ever catch one?"

Brian swung his legs around and sat up to face me. "No, but I saw one once. Annabeth's uncle caught it. They had him tied to a tree limb. He was as tall as a man with a head as big as a dinner plate."

Seeing as how I'm serious about my fishing, I wanted to know more. "Golly, what'd they catch him on?"

"Oh, you can't catch those babies on a hook. You've got to dynamite the log. That stuns the fish and you can shoot him in the head with a .410."

"Did they cook him and eat him?"

"I guess," Brian said. "I wouldn't eat it, though. Catfish are bottom feeders. The meat mostly tastes like mud unless they're farm-raised. Those bayou folks eat them though. They'll eat anything." Brian was beginning to look depressed again. I guess he was thinking about Annabeth being bayou folks herself. Suddenly, Brian swung his head around. There stood Emily Faye, just inside the door listening to us talk. "Why don't you just get lost?" he said.

Emily Faye put her fist to her mouth and ran back down the hall.

"Don't you like her?" I asked.

Brian shrugged his shoulders. "I don't like her, or dislike her," he said.

I wondered if I should tell Biggie about that.

Just then, I heard the grown-ups talking as they left the dining room. Lucas Fitzgerald came over to me. "Son, we've got a date," he said. "That is, if you still want to help me at the museum."

I looked at Biggie.

"Sure, you can go," she said. "I'm going to have a little nap, then maybe go exploring in the shops for a while. We've put off our meeting until tomorrow morning."

As Mr. Fitzgerald and I walked across the street to the museum, I saw Rosebud get into the car and drive off. I wondered where he could be going.

7

When we got to the tall red-brick museum building, which Lucas told me had been the original First State Bank, Lucas stopped at the tall marble steps and took a deep breath. "Look around you, boy," he said, sweeping his arms up toward the green trees and blue sky. "It's far too fine a day for messing around with dusty old papers. What say, you and me take a carriage ride around town?"

"Sure!" I couldn't have agreed with him more.

We walked down the sidewalk past little shops and offices, past the post office and a drugstore, until finally we came to the end of the business district. After that, we crossed another street and climbed a hill that took us through a neighborhood of houses, small but old. At the end of the next block, we came to a little park with tall trees, picnic tables, and playground equipment. Back toward the back, I saw a shed, open on three sides, and beside it stood an old gray horse hitched to a black carriage. The carriage had three pairs of seats, one behind the other, and a bench up front for the driver to sit on. A large man wearing a straw hat was giving the horse water from a bucket.

"Hidy, T.C.," Lucas said. "How's business?"

The man looked up and grinned, showing that he had three teeth missing in front. "Slow for a Saturday," he said. "Ask me if I care. The city pays me and Belle here whether we ride or not. Belle was just tellin' me, she'd 'bout as soon stand right here in the shade as to tote a bunch of tourists around."

Lucas laughed. "Reckon whether she'd mind taking me and my friend here for a little spin? This is J.R. Weatherford from over in Job's Crossing, and he's never been to Quincy before."

"Hop aboard." T.C. emptied the bucket and hung it on a hook in the shed, then untied the reins from the hitching post before swinging himself into the driver's seat. "Y'all want the five-buck spin around town or the ten-buck all-you-can-see?"

Lucas looked at me.

"I got nothin' to do," I said.

"The works, then." Lucas threw his cane aboard and hopped into the carriage. I wondered why he carried that cane in the first place. He seemed spry as a cricket to me.

T.C. clicked his teeth and pulled the reins to the left. Belle gave us a sorrowful look, then began to edge toward the path that led through the park. The old buggy creaked and moaned as we bumped over the curb and into the street.

T.C. picked up a little speaker from the seat beside him and commenced telling us in a singsong voice what we were looking at. You could tell he'd told the same story at least a thousand times before.

"On your right, you'll notice the old one-room schoolhouse, built in 1871. It ain't been in use as a school since the early 1900s when the town built the new school over on Kelly Street. The city was about to tear it down and build a parking lot when Miss Hannah Byrd and her sister, Anna, bought it. Now it's home to Hannah's Handmade Fashions. And if you'll look to your left, you'll see the old cotton gin. It's now an artist's studio and gallery."

We went up and down a slew of streets lined with houses and buildings while T.C. droned on about what they used to be and when they were built. Lucas added comments and bits of information to T.C.'s spiel. The rocking of the carriage and the warm sun made me awful sleepy. In fact, I was dern near asleep sitting up, when the carriage turned and started going down a rutty dirt road. Pretty soon, I could see a muddy shallow creek ahead of us. On the opposite side stood a few dilapidated wooden buildings and a dock that was sitting up on a rise of dry land.

"And this," Lucas said, opening his arms wide, "used to teem with activity. This is the riverboat landing. See those buildings over there?" He pointed. "They were all thriving businesses!" His eyes shone as if he could actually see the huge boats swaying in the water and the workmen along the banks loading and unloading cargo.

All I saw was a lonesome tomcat sitting at water's edge hoping to catch a fish. Then, suddenly, the roar of a

69

motor broke the silence, as a Suburban came barreling out from behind one of the old buildings. It was full of teenagers, and I know they were drinking beer, because one of them threw a can out right in front of us, causing poor Belle to rear up. They all laughed their heads off, and as they drove by, I saw a familiar face looking at me from the backseat.

"That was Emily Faye," I said to Lucas.

"You better tell your granny to get you some glasses, boy," Lucas said. "Why that little gal doesn't go anywhere except where her mama tells her to."

I didn't argue, but I knew what I'd seen.

When we got back to the park, the sheriff's car was parked near the shed. Deputy Elmore Wiggs strolled over to the carriage. The sheriff wasn't with him.

"Hidy, sonny," he said.

"Hidy," I said.

"Got a few more questions to ask you about the killin'. Now then, what time was it you said . . ."

"Just a minute, Wiggs." Lucas raised his hand. "This young man shouldn't be questioned without his grand-mother present. And anyway, where is the sheriff? You're not in charge of this investigation."

Deputy Wiggs kicked the dust with the toe of his boot. "Sheriff's in the hospital," he said. "Appendicitis attack."

"Did he tell you to try to question this minor child?"

"No, sir. Not exactly."

Lucas glared down at the deputy. "Then exactly what did he tell you?"

"Well, sir, what he said was, he said I was to ask Miss Biggie to stop by his hospital room and have a little talk with him. Son, would you give your grandmother that message?"

I nodded and hopped down from the carriage.

When we got back to the hotel I ran upstairs to Biggie's room and found her sitting in a chair reading some pamphlets. "I got these at the Chamber of Commerce," she said. "This town certainly has a colorful past." She put the pamphlets on the table beside her. "How was your afternoon?"

"Okay," I said then told her we'd taken a carriage ride instead of working at the museum. "Biggie, I saw that Emily Faye riding around in a car with some boys that were drinking beer. Does that sound like her to you?"

"Nope," Biggie said. "Are you sure it was her?"

"Yes'm."

"Well, it's none of our business," Biggie said. "Anything else happen?"

"Just that we saw that Deputy Wiggs. He says the sheriff's in the hospital with his appendix. He wants you to come visit him."

"Fine." Biggie got up and moved to the dressing table, and commenced combing her hair. "I'd like to have a word with him, too." She looked at me through the mirror. "What do you think of him?"

"The sheriff?"

"Um-hmm."

"He's got hair growing out of his ears. Biggie, are you gonna help solve this murder?"

"Hard to say." Biggie looked at her watch. "Oops, it's almost five. We've just got time to drop by the hospital before supper."

"Do you know where it is, Biggie?"

"Yep. We passed it coming in. It's just a few blocks away. Feel like a walk?"

I nodded and before a cat could lick his fanny, we were out on the sidewalk walking toward the one-story, red-brick hospital.

Biggie pushed open the heavy glass door and walked to the information desk to ask which room the sheriff was in. A large lady with big blond hair pointed down the hall. "Room one-oh-seven," she said.

Biggie tapped on the door of the room, then pushed it open and stuck her head in. Deputy Wiggs was sitting in a chair next to the bed. The sheriff was propped up in bed wearing a pair of red-and-white striped pajamas that didn't quite close over his big belly. His dinner tray still sat on the nightstand next to the bed. It had a small bowl half full of red Jell-O and another of what looked like plain boiled rice.

The sheriff saw me looking. "I know," he said, looking sad. "Pitiful, ain't it?"

I nodded. "Is that all they gave you for supper?"

"Yup. Wiggs, get up and give Miss Biggie your chair—and get that tray out of here. I cain't stand to look at it any more."

After the deputy picked up the tray and left the room, Biggie plopped down in his chair. I went over to the dresser and stood leaning against it.

"So," Biggie said, "I understand you've had surgery."

"Yes, ma'am. Emergency appendectomy. My wife rushed me to the hospital at midnight last night. They had me on the operating table by one."

"My," Biggie said. "You seem to have made a fast recovery."

The sheriff winced as he reached for a water glass with a bent straw in it. "No'm. Recovery's gonna take some time. You see, my appendix had ruptured and I have peritonitis. They're keeping me in here for another few days, then I have to take it easy for six weeks. That's why I asked you to drop by."

"I'm not sure I understand," Biggie said.

Just at that moment, Deputy Wiggs came back into the room carrying his tape recorder. He drug up a straight chair and set the recorder on his knees.

"Put that away, Wiggs," Sheriff Dugger said. "This is off the record." He took a folded sheet of paper out of his pajama pocket and looked at it, frowning. "Mrs. Weatherford, I've been told you're acquainted with Ranger Red Upchurch."

"We've met on several occasions," Biggie said blushing a little. I think Biggie is sweet on the ranger.

"The ranger was my first boss when we were both with the D.P.S.," he said. "I would trust that man with my life. Red Upchurch says you're the smartest woman he's ever met and if I've got any sense at all, I'll get down on my knees and beg you to help on this case."

Biggie nodded. "The ranger and I have worked on one or two cases together."

"Yes, ma'am, that's what he said. Well, here's the deal. Since I'm going to be laid up for a while, I'm asking for your help, and it may be a godsend."

"How's that?"

"Well, it's like this, I'm not from here, doncha know. I come from over in Flower Mound. Know where that is?"

Biggie nodded. "Not too far from here."

"Ma'am, it might as well be Timbuktu as far as these folks are concerned. If your great grandpappy didn't grow up in this town, you're a foreigner. Only reason I got elected sheriff is because it's a job no local would have on a bet. Mostly, what I do is control tourists and the transients staying in the motels out along Highway 20." He licked his lips. "Now then, one of their own has done got themselves killed. That's the first problem I got. Not only that, it's a pretty good bet one of their own did the killin'. Follow my drift?"

"They're not going to tell you diddley."

"Gawd damn! Upchurch was right. You are fast on the uptake."

"So, what do you want me to do?"

"Keep your eyes and ears open. Report back to me. Mrs. Weatherford, I don't have to brief you very much. Red Upchurch says I should just give you your head."

"What do you know so far?" Biggie asked.

The sheriff nodded to Wiggs who took a little notebook out of his pocket and began to talk. "Hmm, let's see. 'Course we had to go out and notify the girl's family. They took it pretty hard, but when we tried to question them about her life here in town, they clammed up. Said she'd picked up biggity ideas since she came to town and they don't hardly know her no more."

The sheriff nodded. "That's right. I reckon the county will have to bury the poor girl, because those sorry Baughs say they don't have the money to hold a funeral. I reckon they're right about that. Old Mule Baugh used to operate a pretty profitable still out in the woods, but since the county voted wet, his income dried up. Now, all he gets is a little from his vegetable stand out by the road. 'Course, they pretty much live off the land out there."

"How about the others?"

"You know as much as I do," the sheriff said. "They all say they didn't know her very well. She did work for Hen Lester a couple of months last summer, but that's all."

"What about the casket salesman?"

"Nothing, so far. I'm waiting for a report from the county up in Arkansas where he came from. I'll have Wiggs let you know what we find out." The sheriff lay back on his pillows and closed his eyes. "That's about it, Mrs. Weatherford."

Biggie stood up. "Call me Biggie," she said.

When we got back to the hotel and walked into the lobby wonderful smells were coming from the back of the hotel. Gumbo! It could only mean one thing. I raced down the hall, through the dining room, and pushed open the swinging doors that led to the kitchen.

Willie Mae was standing at the stove stirring a roux in a big pot. Rosebud, with an apron tied on, was chopping up onions and green peppers and celery on the table; I could smell French bread baking in the oven.

I ran over to Willie Mae and threw my arms around her. "Boy, am I glad to see you!"

Willie Mae looked down at me with what might have been a smile. "I come to help out Miss Mary Ann," she said. "And what did I tell you about running in the house? Get you an apron on and hand me that bowl of shrimps out of the ice box. Then look in the pantry and see do you see any red pepper in there?"

That night, we all sat down and stuffed ourselves with Willie Mae's special seafood gumbo, the best in the whole wide world.

8

"It's a lovely evening." Biggie pushed herself back from the supper table in the dining room and patted her stomach. She had just polished off a big bowl of Willie Mae's famous raisin bread pudding topped off with rum sauce. "I think I'll take a little stroll around town. Anybody else want to go along?"

"I can't go, Biggie," Butch said, brushing crumbs off his black velvet jeans. "I'm meeting Chip, you know, I told you about him. He owns the Gilded Lily Tea Room. We're getting together with some of his friends to watch an old Judy Garland special on video. Don't you just love Judy?"

Biggie nodded. "How about you, Mattie? Feel like some fresh air?"

Miss Mattie made a face. "Can't," she said. "Norman's been having a hissy fit for me to trim his ingrown toenail."

"Well, it hurts," Mr. Thripp whined. "I can't hardly walk without pain."

"Why can't you do it yourself?" I asked.

Mr. Thripp stretched out his long legs and set one of his feet on the chair next to him, then leaned over. He bent over and stretched as hard as he could, but he could just barely touch his toes with his hands. "It's a curse," he said, "the curse of the Thripps. We're all built the same, long legs and short arms."

"Well, I'll be jiggered," Rosebud said, coming in with a tray to clear the table. "If that don't beat Old Billy."

"I have to trim his toenails regularly," Miss Mattie said. "You should have seen that man's feet when we married. He did not have one single pair of socks that didn't have holes in the ends."

"I'd had to go to a size larger shoe. . . ."

"Ee-yew," Butch said. "If y'all don't hush, I'm just gonna to lose all my supper."

Biggie grinned. "How about you, J.R.?"

Frankly, I couldn't wait to get out of there. What I wanted to do was go home, but it didn't look like that was going to happen until me and Biggie found out who the murderer was.

Biggie turned right when we left the hotel and I followed her to the corner. "Hmm, if we go this way," she pointed, "we'll just see the shops, and I covered all them this afternoon. Let's go the other way. That looks like a residential neighborhood."

The sun was setting behind the trees and a cool breeze rustled the leaves on the big oak trees that lined the street. We passed tall Victorian houses with terraced yards and fancy iron fences. Biggie would pause from time to time in front of a house and make comments. "Just look at that birdbath," she said, stopping in front of one house that was painted green with rust-and-cream trim. "What would you think of us getting one of those to go in the middle of the hosta bed in the side yard?"

"I don't know, Biggie. I'm just a kid."

"Sure you are—but you've got your father's good taste."

"Biggie, my daddy rented out porta-potties to construction sites for a living."

"I know, but everybody said he had the prettiest and cleanest portable toilets around. They only went to the finest building projects in Dallas."

"Yes'm," I said.

"So, what do you think about . . ."

"Hey!" a voice boomed out from the front porch of the house. "What are y'all standing around for? Come on in!" Alice LaRue came down the steps holding a pitcher in her hand. She was wearing overalls with a white tee shirt and had no shoes on. "Come on up here. I just made a big pitcher of planter's punch that I'm just dying to share."

Biggie smiled and motioned for me to open the iron gate that led to the yard. I held it open for Biggie and followed her up the front walk, which was shaded by magnolia trees covered with basketball-sized blooms. The front porch was lined with gardenia bushes covered with white flowers and, in front of them, petunias made a solid pink border. Hanging baskets in every color swung between the porch columns.

"My stars, Alice, this place is a regular Garden of

Eden." Biggie took a deep breath. "What kind of gardenias are these? I've never smelled such a heavenly scent."

"Scarlet O'Hara," Alice said. "They are right fine, aren't they. I ordered them out of a catalog." She broke off a blossom and handed it to Biggie.

"I'd love to have a few cuttings from these." Biggie sniffed the flower.

"Anybody comes by here and wants a cutting, they've got it," Alice said. "Hell, what's a garden for if it ain't to share? Ya'll come on in the house." She held the screen door open. "The dern mosquitoes are too bad this year for porch settin'."

If the outside was bright and colorful, the inside was just the opposite. The walls were covered with dark grayish wallpaper, the paneling was brown and, here and there, old-timey studio portraits of Alice's ancestors frowned down on us. A round dark table with a fringed cloth stood in front of a straight stairway that parted the hall in two. Alice led us down the hall at the right of the stair.

"We'll have our drinks in Papa's study," Alice said. "It's the coolest room in the house. Since I'm outside most of the time, I never could see the sense in putting in air-conditioning." She pushed open the door to an even darker room and set the pitcher on a table in front of the fireplace. "Y'all set down anywhere," she said. "I'll just go get the drinks."

I took a seat on a straight chair and Biggie sat in one of the big leather chairs that flanked the table, and when she did I laughed out loud. Did I mention that Biggie's no bigger than a minute? Well, when she flopped down in that chair, she dern near disappeared. Her feet stuck out straight in front of her. "J.R., stop that laughing and help me up," she said. Just as she had situated herself in the straight chair and I had curled myself up in the leather one, Alice came back followed by Emily Faye, who was carrying a tray with a big pitcher of the punch, two empty glasses, and one glass filled with milk. Alice took the milk off the tray and handed it to me. "This is the only thing I had suitable for a kid," she said. "That and Adam's ale. Set the tray on the table and sit yourself, Em."

Emily did as she was told, perching on a stool in front of the hearth and looking like she'd prefer to be anywhere else but here. She wouldn't look at me and I wondered if she knew I'd seen her riding around in that Suburban.

I took a sip. "It's good." And the milk was, ice cold and really creamy.

"I get it from a dairy outside of town," Alice said. "Fifteen percent butterfat." She poured their drinks, ignoring Emily. "Cheers," she said, lifting her glass and almost draining it. She let out a huge sigh and patted her stomach. "What do you think of our town so far, not counting the murder, of course."

"Not counting the murder, it's charming," Biggie said. "Unfortunately, you can never discount murder."

"Right you are." Alice looked serious. "Murder in a town this small reflects on us all. I just hope that outlander of a sheriff has sense enough to clear it up soon."

"Who do you think did it?" Biggie took the bull by the horns.

"Umm." Alice took another slug of punch and leaned over to refill her glass. "Could have been a transient, I guess. That courtyard opens to the alley out back."

Biggie watched as Alice drank down half her glass again, then plowed ahead. "You don't think it might have been someone, uh, closer to her? Like maybe a lover's quarrel?"

"Brian wouldn't do that!" Emily Faye's voice had panic in it, and she looked like a deer caught in the headlights.

Alice sat up straight and glared at Emily. "Shut up, girl. What do you know about anything?" She looked hard at Biggie. "Brian? It's a possibility, I reckon. Tell the truth, I don't know much about the boy since he went off to college. Watched him grow up, of course. Too much of a mama's boy to suit me, if you know what I mean. I like a kid with a little spunk. Of course, you can't blame the kid, I guess, what with that sorry Quinton Quincy up and leaving like he did."

"Who's that?" I asked.

Alice shook the ice cubes in her glass. "His daddy. He left a long time ago, before Brian was born. What had happened, Mary Ann had a hard pregnancy, felt tired all the time, doncha know. Finally, it got so bad she couldn't even get out of bed in the morning. Well, her mama came over to the house to visit one morning and found her that way and, right away, took her to the doctor—old Dr. Buford. He's dead now. Dr. Buford ran some tests and made a diagnosis of multiple sclerosis. He gave her some pills and said go on home and rest, that it could go into remission, or she could just get sicker and sicker."

"How sad," Biggie said.

"Yeah, it was sad all right. But that's not all. The sad part was when Quinton just up and left town. Told Mary Ann he couldn't deal with a sick wife and a new baby.

Mary Ann moved in with her mama and daddy and lived with them right up until the day they died."

"She sure doesn't look sick, now." Biggie held her glass out for more punch.

"Naw. It was a damn miracle." Alice poured. "After Quinton left, Mary Ann got up out of the bed. She hasn't had a bit of trouble since. We all think old Dr. Buford must of made a mistake about the multiple sclerosis."

"Quincy," Biggie said. "Did his family found the town?"

"Not all by themselves." Alice shifted in her chair and reached for the pitcher of rum punch. "Lucas Fitzgerald's folks were early settlers, too—and my old man's family, the LaRues. They owned the first bank in town. I'm not actually from here. I met Mansfield LaRue when he came to Nashville on business. I was a student at Ward-Belmont College. Can you believe that? Yep. I was a well-finished young lady when Manse met me—at least that's what they all thought." She cackled with laughter. "My daddy made a fortune in scrap metal during the war. He was a junk man! Oh, I was a wild one when Manse married me. Manse didn't care though. He loved me until the day he fell over dead down at the bank. It was an aneurysm, the doctor said. His poor old brain just exploded. He never even knew what hit him."

"Whatever happened to Quinton?"

"Last anybody heard, he was out in California some-where. Got himself a whole new family, so they say. Brian was a pretty angry kid growing up, as he had every right to be. Once I had to stop him from beating his little dog with a stick. But then he went off to school and seemed to be doing better. When he started going out with Anna-beth, he turned into a regular pussycat."

Emily made a noise that sounded like a snort.

"You shut your mouth, girl," Alice snapped. "You'll never get a man, and you know it, least of all a cute kid like Brian."

Emily stuck out her tongue at her mama, just like a little kid would do.

"Do you think his anger could have come back? Brian's, I mean. Enough for him to kill?"

"Hmm. I suppose it's possible. He did say he had a snootful when they got home from that dance."

"Uh-uh," I said.

Biggie looked at me. "What?"

"Brian didn't do it."

"How do you know so much, sonny?" Alice sniggered.

"Because. I just know he couldn't have hurt her. You should have seen how sad he was afterward."

"J.R.," Biggie said. "You've been around more evil in your life than any little boy ought to be. I blame myself for that. Still, you've seen how the most unlikely persons can turn out to be killers."

"Yes'm, I guess so." But in my heart, I knew Brian didn't do it, and I knew Emily felt the same way because she looked at me and smiled when I said that.

Biggie turned back to Alice. "How about Mary Ann? How did she feel about Brian going out with Annabeth?"

"Okay, I guess. Never said anything against her. Of course, Mary Ann's got no guts at all. Comes from living all her life with her parents and never having to think for herself. She was the sissy type, if you know what I mean. I

84

remember once when we were young marrieds, I got her to go fishing with me. First and last time. I had to bait her hook because she wouldn't touch the worms. And take a fish off a hook? Forget it."

"But Brian would be marrying beneath himself, wouldn't he?"

"Well, that's a fact. Come to think of it, maybe Mary Ann did have some resentment toward the girl. Still, I can't see her driving a knife into somebody's chest. Nope, she wouldn't have the stomach for it. Forget Mary Ann."

"And Lucas?"

"Well, like I said, Lucas's family's been here forever. He granddaddy was the first county judge we had. You can see his picture hanging in the county courtroom. I can remember his daddy, old Judge Quincy. Of course, he was old when I came here. Everybody says he was a fine man. Served in the legislature under both Fergusons, Jim and "Ma." When the judge came back from Austin, he did most of the lawyer work for the whole town. He wasn't never a judge. That's just a title of respect folks bestowed on him. They say a more honest man never drew a breath. Lucas, he went to law school because his daddy wanted it, but if you ask me, he'd have preferred to be a college professor, or some such thing. His real love is history, and most especially, the history of this here little town. If you ask me, he's gone overboard about it. Wants to catalog every damn thing that's ever happened around here."

"Do you think he could be capable of murder?" Biggie looked hard at Alice.

"Lucas? Hell, no. He's too feeble. Wouldn't have the

strength to drive the knife home. The man's eighty-three for God's sake! Besides, why?"

"Suppose he didn't want the Quincy family blood to be corrupted by Baugh blood," Biggie suggested.

"That's reaching," Alice said. "Still . . . Lucas *is* a nut when it comes to this town. Keeps his mind too much in the past. Hmm, I'll have to think about that."

"And Hen Lester?" Biggie asked.

"Aw, hell! That woman's dull as ditch water. You want to know anything about her, you'll have to ask her yourself. Still and all, she never liked the girl. Never missed a chance to bad-mouth her. I put it down to pure-dee snobbery, but there might have been some other reason she didn't like the kid."

"What can you tell me about Annabeth's family?" Biggie set her empty glass on the table.

Alice's face froze. "Not a damn thing. More punch?"

Biggie shook her head. "I had the impression that the Baughs had been in this county for a long time."

"County folks and town folks don't mix," Alice said. "Can we change the subject?"

"Strange," Biggie said. "This being a small county, and all. Over in Kemp County, everybody knows everybody else. Do you know how Mary Ann happened to hire Annabeth?"

"Nope. Haven't the foggiest."

Alice looked down at her glass, then drained it. She was kind of wobbly when she stood up and led us out of the room. "Hate to rush y'all off, but the sun's down, and I go to bed with the chickens. Take these glasses out to the kitchen, Em." She weaved her way down the hall and all but pushed us out the front door. "Bye, now. I'll see you in the morning at the hotel."

Before a cat could lick his fanny, the door had slammed behind us and we were standing out on the sidewalk in front of the house.

9

When we got back to the hotel, the moon was rising over the store buildings across the street. Brian and two of his friends were sitting in rocking chairs out front. I took a seat on a cement bench.

"Hey, J.R." Brian looked glum.

"Hey."

"Hey, dude," said one of the guys, who had one brown curl falling over his forehead. "I'm Jason and this here's Matt. We're, like, tryin' to cheer old Brian up, but he ain't havin' any. Tell him he ought to go get a beer with us."

The kid named Matt, who had a real cool earring, said, "Tell him there's plenty of women out there. All he's gotta do is give um a chance. I bet you get all the women you want, huh, kid?"

"I do okay," I said, trying to be cool.

They thought that was very funny, and I turned red.

"Come on, man." Jason gave Brian a shake. "Ain't nobody here but a bunch of old folks. We'll even take the kid with us."

"Okay," Brian said. "You guys are going to hang around until I do. But J.R. can't go."

"Yes I can," I said. "I'll go tell Biggie . . ."

"No," Brian said. "Where we're going's no place for a kid. See you later, J.R."

With that, they all got up and ambled off down the sidewalk. I hoped the beer would make him feel better. I didn't care what the others thought; I knew Brian couldn't hurt a flea. Alice must have been making it up when she said he mistreated his dog.

Inside, things were pretty quiet. Lucas Fitzgerald was sitting in an easy chair beside a potted palm in the lobby reading a book and smoking a cigar. A glass of brandy sat on a little table beside the chair. Mary Ann and Lew Masters were sitting on one of the couches watching *60 Minutes* on television, which surprised me a good bit because I never knew they had a TV in that lobby. It had been hidden behind an antique Chinese screen. Biggie sat down and started watching it with them.

Personally, I think *60 Minutes* is probably the most boring show on TV, so I strolled into the kitchen to look for Willie Mae and Rosebud. I found Willie Mae rolling out a batch of cinnamon rolls. She sprinkled the dough with cinnamon and sugar, then put little dabs of butter on top. After that, she rolled the dough into a big cigar shape and, with a knife, sliced off big, fat cinnamon rolls, which she placed on a pan. When they were all laid out in rows, she put them under a clean, white dishtowel to rise. Rosebud was sitting at the kitchen table drinking a cup of coffee.

"Boy! Those sure smell good," I said. I sure was glad Willie Mae had agreed to stay here and cook for Miss Mary Ann as long as we were here. Nobody makes cinnamon rolls like Willie Mae.

"They for breakfast. Where you been off to?" Willie Mae asked, plopping herself down at the table with a sigh.

"Helping Biggie investigate," I said. "Willie Mae, what happens when the wrong person gets accused of a crime?"

Willie Mae got up and poured me a glass of milk, and set a little plate of cookies beside it. "You have to ask Rosebud that. I don't have no truck with the law."

"Been there many times," Rosebud said. "And it ain't a happy place."

"Humph," Willie Mae said.

"How come you askin', boy?" Rosebud pulled a cigar out of his pocket and sniffed it.

"They're trying to say Brian killed Annabeth, and I know he wouldn't do that. That old Alice LaRue is trying to say he might have done it because she saw him beating his dog once when he was little. Does that make any sense to you, Rosebud?"

"Puts me in mind of my cousin, Daniel P. Trahan," Rosebud said, pulling out his big Zippo lighter.

"You ain't lightin' that cigar in this kitchen," Willie Mae said.

Rosebud grinned. "Come on, son. We'll go out in the courtyard and I'll tell you about Daniel P. while I smoke my cigar in peace."

I finished my milk and stuck two cookies in my pocket. "Ain't—I mean isn't it still roped off?"

"Nope. The sheriff took the tape down this afternoon. Said he'd gathered all the evidence he needed."

Rosebud headed down the hall to the French doors that led to the courtyard. I followed. We found a seat on a bench and Rosebud lit his cigar, taking a deep draw. He blew out three perfect smoke rings.

"What happened to Daniel P.?" I asked.

"Wellsir, it went this way." Rosebud leaned back and crossed his legs, looking up at the moon. "Daniel P. wasn't really my cousin, doncha know. My Auntie Blanche found him amongst the cypress knees down in Big Mamou when he wasn't no bigger than a possum. He was wrapped up in a old dirty blanket and settin' in a washtub."

"His mama had just left him there?"

"Yeah." Rosebud blew another smoke ring. "Wellsir, Auntie Blanche, she taken him home and took good care of the little feller. In time, she came to love him like he was her own. Thing was, as he grew older, old Daniel P. kept on asking 'Who my momma? Who my momma?' All the time he kept askin' that same question. Auntie Blanche, she say, 'Who feed you all the crawfish pie you can hold? Who stitch up the fine clothes you wear? Who nurse you back to health when you sick with the gallopin' croup? Nobody but me, that's who.' But Daniel P., he just keep askin' 'Who my momma?' and then 'Where my momma?' "

"What was wrong with him? Seems like he'd of been grateful."

"Don't it? Well, things went on like that until Daniel P.

91

was about six. 'Long about that time, he found a little old stray hound dog somebody had dumped out beside the road. He brought it home, and when Auntie Blanche said he could keep him, Daniel P. washed him and fed him 'til that dog was fat and fine. Old Barney, that was his name, turned out to be the best coon dog in the parish. Ooo-wee, that boy was proud. Go in the kitchen and bring me out a glass of sweet milk."

I ran in the kitchen and, when I came back with the milk, Rosebud took a big swig, then continued. "Wellsir, one morning, bright and early, Daniel P. got out of bed, taken up his gun and went out the back door, hollering for Barney. He hollered and he whistled, but old Barney, he never came. Daniel P. never saw that dog again."

"Poor Daniel P.," I said. "Did he get him another dog?"

"Nope. Never wanted another dog. It was after that that Daniel P. took to robbing birds' nests and smashing the eggs and runnin' after Auntie Blanche's hens 'til the poor things would fall over from exhaustion. Once, he tied two of her kittens' tails together with baling wire and throw'd um over the clothesline. The poor little things dern near clawed each other to death."

"I don't think I like him much."

"Wasn't much to like. Well, when Daniel P. come to be about fourteen or so, he fell in love with Maydella LeJeune, a girl he met at school, and she said she loved him back. Ooo-wee, Daniel P. seemed like he changed overnight. He was kind to animals and sweet as sugar to Auntie Blanche, who told all her friends it was a miracle."

"Love did that?"

"Yep."

"So, what happened?"

"Nothin' much except Maydella found her another feller, Artis Johnson, who was a big strappin' guy who could run, shoot, and fight rings around poor old Daniel P."

"So, then what happened to Daniel P?"

"Oh, he's in Angola Prison now. Been there might' near all his life. 'Bout ten years ago, he found the Lord, so now he sets in his cell most of the time readin' his Bible and prayin' for forgiveness for shootin' Artis Johnson in the back of the head with a 12-gauge shotgun."

"I don't like that story."

"They can't all be pretty. But if you listen real good, you might just learn something." Rosebud got up and brushed off the front of his trousers.

"Rosebud, sit back down," I said. "What's that story got to do with Brian?"

"All I'm sayin' is that once a feller's momma or papa runs off and leaves him, sometimes he don't feel too good about himself. Some can take it—others can't. Daniel P. just didn't handle it too good is all."

"And then when that girl dumped him, that was the last straw. Right?"

"Right."

"So, you're saying Brian could be the same way?"

"Could be."

"I'll have to think about that. Hey, look Rosebud. There goes a white possum!"

Rosebud looked where I was pointing. "Sure is," he said. "If you can catch him, he'll give you three wishes."

I didn't believe that, but I took out after the possum anyway. Possums can't run very fast, and they're dumb as dirt, but they can turn on a dime. I chased him across the courtyard and back, and almost had my hands on him, when I tripped on a loose stone and fell flat on my face. Naturally, Rosebud had to laugh his head off. I ignored him and kept chasing, but just as I was right up on him, he scuttled under the bushes next to the hotel and disappeared down a hole in the foundation.

"Darn!" I said.

I looked around for a stick to poke down the hole when I saw something.

"Look, Rosebud," I called. "Looky here what I found."

What I'd found was a door in the bricks at the base of the building. It wasn't much taller than me and was hidden by the tall shrubs that grew up next to the wall. Rosebud walked over and stood beside me.

"What?" he said. "I don't see nothin'."

"Look right here." I pointed.

Rosebud bent over and examined the little door. "Well, what do you know about that."

"What do you think it's for, Rosebud?" I asked.

"Could be it leads to the cellar, or something. Don't matter much, I reckon. Hey, what's this?" He picked up something white off the ground and held it out for me to see.

"Looks like a lady's purse," I said. "Let's look inside."

Rosebud had already snapped open the clasp and was running his hand inside the bag. He pulled out a little blue billfold. "Come over here by the light so we can see," he said.

We moved over next to the kitchen window and looked at the billfold by the light that shone through.

"Lordy." Rosebud pulled out a driver's license. "This purse belonged to the dead girl."

I looked at the card. Sure enough, printed on the front, bigger'n Dallas, were the words *Annabeth Baugh.*

"You take this in to your Biggie right this very minute," Rosebud said.

I took the purse and ran for the lobby, where I found Biggie sitting on the couch talking to Miss Mary Ann. Mr. Lew Masters was sitting on a chair leaning toward them like he was awfully interested in what they were saying. The TV had been turned off and the Chinese screen pushed back in front of it.

"Biggie!" I said. "Guess what me and Rosebud found. We found . . ."

Biggie turned and glared at me. "J.R. haven't I taught you any manners at all? Grown-ups are talking. Now sit down and wait your turn."

I sat, jiggling the purse on my knees hoping Biggie would notice. She didn't even look at me.

"Now, calm down, honey," she said to Miss Mary Ann. "There's no problem so big that we can't put our heads together and solve it."

"I just don't know how on God's green earth I could have forgotten." Miss Mary Ann's hands fluttered in the air. "What am I going to do? If it was anything besides a wedding, I'd just call the folks and tell them we had a murder on our hands, and they'd have to go somewhere else."

Biggie nodded. "You can't do that to a brand-new bride and groom," she said. "Besides, where else would they go in this little town?"

"That's just it!" Miss Mary Ann's voice rose. "The only other place with enough room would be the Surrey House Inn where the Rotary and Kiwanas Clubs meet. But they're not fancy enough to cater a wedding brunch. My soul, they'd probably serve meatloaf and canned green beans."

Biggie stood up. "Well, the first thing we need to do is go out to the kitchen and talk to Willie Mae. Then we can inventory the supplies on hand and try to make up a menu."

Miss Mary Ann seemed to relax a little and Mr. Masters reached across his knees and squeezed her hand. She smiled weakly at him, then stood up and followed Biggie back to the kitchen. I trailed along, swinging the purse beside me.

"How many you 'spectin'?" Willie Mae asked after they explained the problem to her.

"Twenty counting the bride and groom," Miss Mary Ann said. "They wanted to eat in the courtyard, but under the circumstances . . ."

"What you want to serve?" Willie Mae interrupted.

"Oh!" Miss Mary Ann jumped up from the table where she had been sitting. She went over to her little desk by the window and pulled a slip of paper out of a basket. "Here's the menu they asked for. Let's see, quiche with Brie and baby shrimp, fruit salad with poppy seed dressing on a bed of baby field greens, angel biscuits with sliced ham, and Lane cake for dessert."

Biggie got up and poured herself a cup of coffee from the pot on the stove.

"You ain't gonna get a wink's sleep tonight," Willie Mae said.

"Oh, yes I will." Biggie spooned sugar in her coffee. "After Alice LaRue's planter's punch, I'm falling asleep on my feet this very minute. Now, Mary Ann, what time are they scheduled to eat?"

"Twelve noon!" Miss Mary Ann wrung her hands. "We'll never make it!"

"We can, if we get us some help," Willie Mae said. "You got anybody you can call?"

"Well . . . Hen Lester owes me a favor. I catered her daughter's sweet sixteen party on one day's notice. She was taking the girls to Shreveport for lunch and a show, but the weather turned off bad. She was so grateful at the time, she promised to pay me back if I ever needed her. . . ."

"It's payback time," Biggie said. "Go call her right now. In the meantime, we'd better all be off to bed. Tomorrow's going to be a busy day."

I stood behind Biggie while she turned the key in her door. "J.R., what are you doing here? It's late."

I followed her into her room and held the purse high for her to see.

"What's that?"

"It's Annabeth's purse. Me and Rosebud found it out in the courtyard, right next to the little-bitty door."

Biggie took the purse and sat down on the bed. "What little-bitty door?" She didn't look at me.

"There's a little door that goes into the side of the house. It's hid behind some bushes."

"Hmmm," Biggie said. It was clear she wasn't interested in the little door. She pulled a blue slip of paper out of the pocket inside the purse and looked at it, frowning. "What in the world . . ."

"What is it, Biggie?"

"It's a check," Biggie said, "a check from Hen Lester to Annabeth for one hundred dollars! What in the world do you suppose this is for?"

I shrugged.

"We've got to take this to the sheriff tomorrow," she said, snapping the little purse shut, "just as soon as we get done with the wedding party." She reached over and gave me a hug. "You did good, honey. Now, scoot off to bed. We've got a big day ahead of us."

10

Rosebud knocked on my door bright and early the next morning. "Get up," he called. "Miss Biggie wants you down in the kitchen."

I put my pillow over my head and pretended not to hear. Everything was quiet. I breathed a sigh of relief, thinking Rosebud must have gone on off. I went back to dreaming the dream I'd been having about a giant dog kicking a boy. The boy was rolled up in a ball on the ground trying to cover his head, but the dog kept on kicking him with his back legs. Finally, the dog stopped kicking the boy and raised up his hind leg and went to the bathroom on the boy's feet. That's when I woke up. Something wet was running down my feet, which had been sticking out from under my blanket. I sat up. There was Rosebud, grinning like a cat eating briers and pouring water from a paper cup on my feet.

"Ee-yew," I said. "Quit that!"

Rosebud just grinned and walked to the door. "Get up," he said. "Your Biggie wants you in the kitchen."

Well, as you might imagine, I was in a pretty bad mood when I got downstairs—not that anybody cared. Biggie and Mrs. Hen Lester were seated at the kitchen table chopping raisins and cherries for the Lane cake. Miss Mary Ann was arranging pink roses and baby's breath in crystal vases at a table next to the wall while Willie Mae stood at the counter rolling out piecrusts. Even Lew Masters was helping. He was cutting the rind off a big wheel of Brie cheese.

"Get you a cinnamon roll off the stove," Willie Mae said over her shoulder. "Then I want you to peel these here shrimp in the sink."

I poured myself a glass of milk from the fridge and took two cinnamon rolls off the pan on the stove. "Can I go outside and eat these?"

"Sure," Biggie said. "Just make sure you come back. We need all hands on deck."

I went out into the courtyard and sat on a bench. I thought about the dream I'd been having. I was pretty sure it had something to do with Brian and Rosebud's cousin, Daniel P. Both of them had been mean to dogs because someone important had gone off and left them. At least that's what everybody seemed to think. Well, plenty of people had left me. First my daddy died, then my mama shipped me off to live with Biggie on account of she couldn't take care of me, her being high-strung and all. But, try as I might, I couldn't think of one single reason why a thing like that would make a person mean to animals. I was nice to animals. Well, all except Prissy Moody, the poodle who lives next door to us and is really obnoxious. And all I'd ever done to Prissy was to tease her a little. I just didn't understand it. I shrugged my shoulders and popped the last bite of cinnamon roll in my mouth. Maybe Biggie's right. She says I think too much, just like my daddy, who was a very deep person although not many people knew that about him because he kept it hidden behind a devil-may-care attitude. Biggie said that, not me. Myself, I can't hardly remember my daddy.

I got up and went back into the kitchen, where Willie Mae tied an apron around my waist and set me to peeling shrimp at the sink. They were little-bitty, the kind that, when you take the heads off, there's not much left. "This will take all day," I said. "Where's Butch and the Thripps? Why aren't they helping?"

"They've gone over to Shreveport to them gambling boats," Willie Mae said. "Don't let none of them shells go down the sink."

Peeling shrimp is a slow and stinky business. Some shrimps let go of their shells real easy; others stick on like glue and you sometimes have to tear up the shrimp to get the shell off. I was concentrating on my work and not paying much attention to what the others were saying until I heard a loud crash and a scream. Miss Mary Ann had dropped a vase on the floor and the glass had shattered. When she bent down to pick it up, she cut her finger real bad.

"Now look what I've gone and done." She stared at her finger while the blood dripped on the floor.

Willie Mae dried her hands with a clean towel and

came over to examine the cut. "Come on in here with me," she said, leading Miss Mary Ann out toward the dining room. "I've got some salve in my room that'll fix you right up."

"I'm just nervous, that's all," Miss Mary Ann said. "Lord, lately, seems like I can't do anything right."

"Now, hon, that's just not so." Lew Masters came over to give her a quick hug. "You go with Willie Mae. I'll clean up this mess while you're gone."

I watched while he got the broom from the closet and swept up the broken glass.

"Take a damp paper towel and wipe down the area after you sweep," Biggie said. "It will take up all the little slivers."

"Is that so?" Hen Lester said. "I never heard that."

Biggie nodded. "I learned it from Willie Mae."

"Willie Mae knows everything," I said. "Biggie, these shrimp are hard to peel."

"I know," Biggie said. "We all have our crosses to bear."

"Biggie, stop teasing."

Biggie ignored me. She was asking Hen about Annabeth. "What can you tell me about the girl? Anything you can remember might be helpful—even if it seems unimportant."

"Well, let me see." Hen got up and washed the sticky off her hands. She picked up a Baggie filled with pecan halves and brought them back to the table. "They're a strange family; keep to themselves. They live out by Caddo Lake, nothing but a tumbledown old farm house and some ratty outbuildings. The old man and old lady had a raft of children. Some went off from home, but a few still live there with the parents. I heard the oldest boy got sent to the pen for something, I forget what. And, let me see, it seems there was a girl, lots younger than the others, retarded I think." She laughed. "Of course, they're all so dumb, I don't see how they could tell." She poured the pecans out in a pile on the table and commenced breaking them up with her fingers and putting them in a Pyrex bowl. "They've lived in the county for generations, but because they're country folks, we don't have much to do with them. Not that there's anything wrong with living in the country, you understand. Nowadays, it's gotten quite chic to own a country place. But back in the old days, well, most country people were farmers and not very well educated, if you know what I mean."

Biggie opened her mouth to say something, then closed it with a snap. She nodded and waited for Hen to say more.

"When I was a child," Hen said, "I used to see them come into town on a Saturday. The old man would be driving the wagon. The back would be piled high with animal pelts and kids. He was a trapper, you see. That was back before every creature that walks the woods was an endangered species." She curled her lip when she said that.

"Would that be Annabeth's father?"

"Oh, my no. That must have been her grandfather. My soul, he was old back when I was just a tot. Her father may not have even been born then. And there was always a woman with him, a wife—or sister, I don't know what. I do know she was crazy, or retarded, or something. I do

103

remember that. I only saw her once. She was riding on the wagon with the kids, her bare legs hanging out the back. She wore nothing but a feed sack with holes cut for the arms and head. It wasn't even sewed into a dress—just a plain old Burress Mills feed sack with the label still on it. And her hair was down to her waist, gray and wild. My mama took me by the hand and yanked me into the drugstore before I got a very good look. When we got home, I asked Mama about the woman and she said she was just a poor old crazy lady, and I should feel sorry for her. Later I heard Mama and Papa talking, and they were saying how beautiful she used to be when she was young and what a shame it was."

"What was?" Biggie asked.

"That's what I asked." Hen pushed the Pyrex bowl toward the middle of the table. "But they never would tell me. It's funny, I haven't thought about that incident until this very day. What do you suppose they meant?"

"I don't know," Biggie said. "But I have a feeling it might be important. By the way, do you know any reason Alice LaRue might not want to talk about the Baughs?"

"Alice not want to talk about them?" Hen Lester laughed. "Why, Alice has something to say about any and everything. Ooh, I just thought of something else. I don't guess it's important, though. Isn't it funny how, when you get to talking about things that happened long ago, memories you'd forgotten come popping back in your head?"

Biggie nodded. "Everything is important. What was it you remembered?"

"Well, I was just a little girl, playing with my paper dolls in the parlor after dinner. Papa was reading, and Mama was listening to *One Man's Family* on the radio. Remember that show?"

Biggie put down her knife and nodded again. "Go on."

"Well, Mama waited until the commercial came on, then turned down the radio and turned to Papa. 'Lloyd,' she said. 'Lloyd, I heard something right strange at Missionary Society today.' Papa, of course, never liked to be interrupted in his reading, but he put his finger in his place and closed the book. Well, Mama went on to tell about how the church ladies were getting up Christmas boxes for poor families and they were fixing one for the Baughs out by the lake. Papa looked impatient like he was prone to do when Mama took a long time getting to the point."

Personally, I thought Mrs. Lester was doing a pretty good job of making a short story long, but Biggie just kept waiting for her to get to the point.

"Anyway, what Mama had to say was that some of the ladies were saying that the Baughs had found Diamond Lucy's baby and taken it to raise. They said that the crazy lady was that child. Maybe Lucas is right and they are descendants of Diamond Lucy."

"Could be, I suppose," Biggie said. "Still, I don't think Diamond Lucy's baby would still be alive when you were a child."

"Well, that's probably right. I never thought of that. Still, if it were true, it could explain why some, like Annabeth and that woman, turned out pretty while the others are ugly as mud." Hen Lester set down her knife. "Do you think we should pour the fruit and nuts in a bowl together, or let Willie Mae do it?"

Biggie got up and found a large bowl in the cabinet. "Let's mix it in . . ."

"Stop!" Willie Mae had just come back into the kitchen. "You gonna make a mess. I got to sprinkle sugar and flour on them fruits so they won't all be stuck together. Y'all go on out in the dining room and get the flowers ready. I'll finish the cooking."

I stepped away from the sink and started to take off my apron.

"Where you goin'?" Willie Mae had scooped up the bowl of fruit and was wiping the table with a rag. "You just set your fine self down here and start takin' the veins outta them shrimps. Here, use this knife—and don't cut yourself. After you get through with that, I need for you to grate up this fresh coconut for the cake. After that, you needs to go out in the courtyard and help Rosebud sweep." She opened the oven door and took out a pan of little tiny angel biscuits, which she set on the table. Next, she took a baked ham out of the fridge and set it beside the biscuits. "Mr. Lew, I reckon you better take this here knife and start slicing up that ham. Thin slices now. No, not like that. Lemme show you." She took the knife from him and cut off a slice so thin you could pretty near see through it."

Lew Masters tried again, and finally got one that satisfied Willie Mae, who then turned to Biggie. "Now, then, Miss Biggie, you open these here biscuits and put a piece of ham in each one. No, not hanging over the sides like that. Fold it first. There, I reckon that'll have to do. Miss Hen, you'd best finish them flowers Miss Mary Ann done started."

We worked for about five minutes without talking, then Biggie, setting a ham biscuit on the silver tray Willie Mae had provided, turned to Mr. Masters. "I guess one of these days soon, you and Mary Ann will be having a wedding party."

Mr. Masters looked sad. "I can only hope and pray," he said.

"I'm surprised," Biggie said. "You obviously care for her, and she seems fond of you. What could stop you from marrying?"

"Many things." Mr. Masters put down his knife. "Is this enough ham, Miss Willie Mae?" When Willie Mae nodded, he turned back to Biggie. "For one thing, you may not know it, but Mary Ann was abandoned by her first husband, that worm, Quinton Quincy. Even though I've told her I'll be true to her until death, she has trouble believing me. She says she doesn't know whether she can ever trust a man again. Frankly, I don't know what to do. I'd do anything to prove my love for her."

Biggie patted his shoulder. "Don't worry, honey. Right now, she's worried about the murder, and how Brian's taking it. If you've never been a mother, you couldn't understand a mother's feelings. I'm sure she'll come around. I've seen the way she looks at you."

"Really? You think she cares?"

"Sure!" Biggie said. "Just give her time."

"Oh, I will, Miss Biggie, all the time in the world. I'll wait for her forever."

"That's the spirit." Biggie got up and went to the fridge, and took out a bowl of washed parsley. She began putting it around the tray of ham biscuits for a garnish. "How are we doing, Willie Mae?"

"We gonna make it." Willie Mae was beating batter for the Lane cake.

And, somehow, it did all get done. Before the wedding party arrived from the church, I took a peep out at the courtyard. A long buffet table had been set up next to the ivy-covered wall. It was spread with a pink cloth and in the middle stood a big silver bowl full of pink roses with fern leaves and baby's breath. Silver trays were piled high with quiche and ham biscuits. A crystal bowl held fruit salad with a smaller bowl full of poppy seed dressing next to it. And, right in the middle, stood a four-layer Lane cake covered in white icing. All around the base of the cake was a wreath of sugared fruit: strawberries, green grapes, kumquats, and black cherries. It was the most beautiful cake I'd ever seen. Another table was set up with bottles of champagne iced down in a big silver punch-bowl. I glanced around at the smaller tables, also with pink cloths and rose bouquets in little silver vases. These were for the people to sit at while they ate. I looked at the fountain with its statue of a young girl. Somebody had floated white gardenias all over the top of the water. It was beautiful. I wondered what the wedding guests would think if they knew that just two nights ago, Anna-beth Baugh had lay dead in that very fountain.

11

The guests started arriving at twelve. The bride wasn't even a girl. She was an old gray-headed lady, and her new husband had a bald head and a red face and talked real loud. Miss Mary Ann, who had come out of her room wearing a pink lace dress, greeted them at the door and led them out to the courtyard where they all made a big deal about how pretty everything looked. Rosebud and I watched through the French doors while they toasted the bride and groom. After that, the bride tossed her wedding bouquet over her head. I like to died when two of the women guests butted their heads together and fell on top of each other trying to get their hands on the thing. One large lady's dress flew over her head so high you could see her underpants. I looked at Rosebud to see if he'd seen, and it was pretty clear he had, because he was doubled over laughing into his blue bandanna handkerchief. I slapped my hands over my mouth to keep the giggles in, and took off for Biggie's room to tell her what she'd missed.

I found her sitting on her bed with the contents of Annabeth's purse dumped out on the pink coverlet. I took a seat on the other side of the bed and watched while she picked up a little silk bag with a drawstring tie and pulled the top open. She put her fingers inside and pulled out a gold lipstick, a plastic powder compact, and a little vial of perfume, the kind they give away at department stores. Biggie opened the perfume and smelled it, then made a face. Next, she opened Annabeth's billfold and took everything out. "Let's see," she said, "according to this, she was eighteen years old in May. She was five-foot-two and weighed ninety-eight pounds."

"About your size, Biggie." I picked up the empty purse and began tossing it up and catching it.

"Don't do that. Nope, I weigh a hundred and twelve. Here's a library card, a credit card from Penney's, and someone's business card." She held it out as far as she could and squinted at it. "Hmm, Texas Department of Mental Health and Mental Retardation, and there's a local address and phone number." She turned the card over. "Someone's written a date and time on the back. Tomorrow at 10:00 A.M. Wonder why she was carrying that around."

"I don't know, Biggie." I squinted at the card. "I reckon she might have had an appointment for that time."

"Most likely—and I'm going to have to find out why. Well, hand me the purse. We might as well put these things back." She looked at her watch. "My soul, it's nearly two. I'm hungry enough to eat fried buzzard."

I picked up the purse to hand it back to Biggie, and when I did, I heard a rustling sound, like paper. I opened it up and felt something between the silk lining and the leather outside. "Biggie, there's something in here."

Biggie took the purse and ran her finger behind the lining. "It's come loose," she said. "And, you're right. There's something in here. I can't quite reach it. Hand me my manicure scissors off the dresser."

I got the scissors and Biggie began clipping the threads that held the lining in place. "Ah," she said. "I've got it." She pulled out a folded slip of paper about the size of my hand. This is what she read out loud to me: *Go back where you came from if you know what's good for you.* And it's signed, *The Angel of Death.*

"Wow," I breathed, "that's spooky. Biggie, what do you . . ."

But I could have saved my breath, because Biggie was already stuffing the stuff back in the purse and looping her own purse over her arm. "Come on," she said. "We've got to take this to the hospital and show it to the sheriff, but first let's have some lunch. Hand me my little address book off the night table. I've got an idea."

When we got downstairs, the folks that were staying at the hotel had gathered around the long table in the dining room. Platters of ham sandwiches sat on each end of the table along with pitchers of iced tea. Willie Mae had saved us a bowl of fruit salad from the wedding party and had even made a small Lane cake just for us.

"Y'all come on in and have a seat," Miss Mary Ann said, starting to get up.

"Keep your seat," Biggie said. "You must be worn to a frazzle. How'd the wedding party go?"

"Great," said Lew Masters, who was chewing on a ham sandwich. "This little lady sure knows how to throw a party."

Miss Mary Ann ducked her head and blushed while I was thinking about how the rest of us had done most of the work.

Butch sat at one end of the table wearing a red sequin-covered baseball cap, a big grin plastered all over his face. Miss Mattie and Norman Thripp sat side by side next to him. Mr. Thripp's face was longer than a plow mule's, while Miss Mattie frowned and refused to look in his direction.

"Lordy mercy." Biggie pulled out a chair and sat down next to Rosebud. "Y'all didn't stay long at the gambling boats. Did they take all your money so soon?"

"Not me, Biggie." Butch pulled a fat wad of bills out of his pocket. "See this. All twenties. I've got four hundred and forty dollars here." He fanned out the bills so we could all see. He pointed to his head. "I got this cap at the gift shop. Biggie, you should go over there. They have the cutest things!"

"Humph," Miss Mattie said.

"Uh-oh," I said. "Did you lose the tearoom?"

"Of course not," Miss Mattie said. "Just our whole savings account."

Mr. Thripp seemed to shrink down in his chair.

"Not that I had a thing to do with it," Miss Mattie went on. "I got tired and went down to the restaurant. Norman just kept on dropping those quarters in the machines like he was some big high roller. Finally, I went back up to see if I could get everybody to come on let's go home, and there he was, cashing in his last hundred-dollar bill for another big pile of quarters."

"Quarters won't do it," Butch said. "You gotta think big. I was playing the half-dollar machines."

Miss Mattie turned to face Biggie. "Anyway, when do you think we can all go home, Biggie? Me and Norman are losing money every day we stay here."

"Why ask me?" Biggie said.

"Because, you have influence. Now, Biggie, don't try to tell me you don't because I know better." Norman tried to look stern. "We want you to go to that sheriff and tell him we didn't have one thing to do with those murders." He gave up on looking stern. "Will you, Biggie? Please?"

"Me, too," Butch said. "Heather Fortenberry's wedding is coming up in three weeks, and I haven't even ordered the flowers. Of course, old Brother Fortenberry is so cheap, he wants to use white carnations for the bridal bouquet. Is that tacky, or what?"

"Real tacky," Miss Mattie said. "Ruby Muckleroy says Meredith Michelle is going to have white orchids when she gets married." She giggled. "If she ever does, that is."

"Oh, she'll get married all right," Butch said. "She's going to drag Paul and Silas Wooten to the alter, or I miss my guess. Then she'll be your cousin, Biggie."

"Maybe." Biggie grinned. "We'll deal with that back in

113

Job's Crossing. In the meantime, I want to make sure I have the addresses and phone numbers of our new friends here in Quincy." She took her address book out of her purse. "Lucas, would you mind entering yours in my book?"

"Gladly." Lucas wrote quickly in the book and looked at Biggie. "I know the addresses of the other society members. Would you like me to enter them?"

"Nope," Biggie said, taking the book and passing it over to Miss Mary Ann and Mr. Masters. "I'll ask them later." She waited until the others had signed and then put the book back in her purse and pushed her chair back. "Come, J.R., we have an errand to do."

As we were leaving the hotel, we met the other members of the historical society coming in the front.

"We couldn't stay away," Hen said. "We just had to know how the wedding went."

"Were there any refreshments left?" Alice LaRue wanted to know. "I heard you had a Lane cake. My mama used to make those every single Christmas. Haven't tasted one in a coon's age."

"There's plenty left," Biggie said. "But, first, I have a favor to ask of you." She took out her little address book. "Would you all sign my book? Put in your addresses and phone numbers. I don't want to go back home without them."

"Why sure, Biggie," Hen said. "And we want yours, too."

Alice took the pen and scrawled some words in the book. "Em has her own phone for some reason. Just had a wall-eyed fit until I had it put in. I don't guess you'd care to have hers?"

"Never mind that," Biggie said. "I'll ask her myself when I see her."

"Suit yourself," Alice said, handing the book to Hen.

When we got to the hospital, we found the same lady with the large blond hair sitting at the volunteer's desk. She was reading a hospital chart and scratching her head with the point of a yellow pencil. She jumped and shoved the chart under the desk when we walked up.

"Is it all right if we drop in on Sheriff Dugger?" Biggie asked.

"You could if he was still here." The woman shrugged her shoulders. "The thing is, he just up and left about an hour ago."

"He left?" Biggie raised her eyebrows. "I thought he was to stay a few days more."

"He was supposed to. Young Dr. Littlejohn was fit to be tied, said he wouldn't be responsible if his stitches came undone, but the sheriff didn't pay him any mind— just said he had things to do. He put on his clothes and Elmore Wiggs helped him out to the police car." She pronounced it PO-lice car.

"Can you tell me where he lives?" Biggie asked.

"I could, but it wouldn't do you a speck of good. He said he was going straight down to his office and work on that murder case. You hear about that?"

Biggie nodded. "Thanks for your help," she said, turning and heading out the door.

The sheriff's office was in a square concrete block building next to the courthouse. We found Sheriff Dugger and Deputy Wiggs hunched over a computer monitor.

The sheriff pointed to the screen. "Now what the hell do you suppose that means?"

Deputy Wiggs scratched his head but didn't answer.

"Afternoon, boys," Biggie said. "Having computer problems?"

The sheriff eased his chair around to face Biggie, holding on to his side. "Howdy, ma'am." He gestured toward the screen. "This machine ain't been nothin' *but* a problem since that fuzzy-cheeked little county attorney talked the commissioners into puttin' it in here."

The deputy spoke up in a voice that sounded like a whiny girl. "We told um we didn't want it. But they wouldn't listen. Said they wanted to bring this county into the twenty-first century."

"Hell, it'll take more than a damn ('scuse me ma'am) computer to do that!"

"As far as I can tell," Biggie said, taking a seat in the oak swivel chair opposite the desk, "this town is locked in the nineteenth century. The only thing these people are interested in is the past. But, the truth is, we have a very present problem on our hands, and that's the murder of Annabeth Baugh." She pulled the little white purse out of her big black one and pushed it across the desk toward the sheriff. "J.R. found this in the courtyard last night."

"No problem." The sheriff picked up the purse and dumped its contents, including the note, onto the desk.

"It belonged to Annabeth," Biggie said. "Read the note first."

The sheriff read the note and blew out a loud puff of air. He looked at Biggie. "Can't see how my boys overlooked this," he said. "What do you make of this note?"

Biggie wriggled in the chair, which was too big for her. "Well, I think this eliminates Brian. He was my first suspect. You know, lovers' quarrel, or some such thing. But this note puts a different light on it. Don't you think so?"

"What makes you think that?"

"Because, if Brian killed her, it would have been a crime of passion coming out of strong emotions, like anger or jealousy. At least that's what I think." Biggie picked up the note. "This note indicates premeditation."

"I suppose," the sheriff said. "What about Mary Ann? Could she have written this note as a way of tryin' to warn the girl off from marryin' her boy? But then we come down to the *why*? What would Mary Ann have had against her?"

"Well, there's this card from MHMR," Biggie said. "Could she have found out Annabeth had some mental problems? No, that wouldn't be enough to cause her to do murder. Besides, she seemed genuinely fond of the girl. I just don't get the impression Mary Ann is all that smart— smart enough to put on such a good act, doncha know."

The sheriff nodded again. "The way I see it, Mary Ann is just a nice lady that's had to make the best of a bad situation."

"Then you've heard about her husband running off and leaving her to raise Brian all by herself?"

"It's a small town, Miss Biggie. Most everybody knows about that."

"Another thing," Biggie said, "when I asked Alice LaRue to tell me about Annabeth's family, she shut up tighter than a twenty-dollar face-lift. Why would she do that?"

"Well, now we have to go back to ancient history. When Miss Alice first came here, as a young bride, they tell she was right nice looking, but wild as javalina. Old Manse couldn't do nothin' with her. She didn't take anymore stock in convention than she does today." The sheriff picked a cigarette out of the open pack on his desk. He lit it and blew out a cloud of yellow smoke. "Well, as the story goes, Alice was plumb crazy about horses, Tennessee walkers. You know, show horses."

Biggie nodded.

"So Manse, he had a little farm out by the lake and he had it fixed up with horse barns and a ridin' ring and all such as that. Then he and Alice went up to Tennessee and bought some fine horses. The idea was, that Alice could breed them. It would give her something to do besides roaring around town in her Cadillac and drinking whiskey with the boys down at the pool hall."

"And it worked?"

"For a while," the sheriff said. "The problem was, Manse had hired Mule Baugh to tend to the horses, muck out the stalls, and feed them, and all."

"Who's that?"

"Well, old Mule, he's Annabeth's daddy, doncha know."

"Oh," Biggie said. "Go on."

"Well, the story goes, that Alice got just a little too friendly with Mule. Took to staying out there all night, and coming home smelling of moonshine and only often enough to change clothes and eat. People started to talk, as they will, and that kind of talk ain't at all good for a banker in a small town. Finally one day, Manse's board

118

members got together with him and told him he'd better do something about his wife because it was hurting business. Some of the bank's big depositors were taking their banking business to Marshall."

"So, what did he do?"

"Nobody knows for sure. All we know is, suddenly the horses were sold, the barn was torn down, and the farm was let out to a tenant who planted the whole thing in sorghum. After that, Alice took up eating and tending her garden. Manse would never let the name of Baugh be mentioned in his house again and woe be unto any Baugh that might have wanted to take out a loan to tide them over until their crops came in."

"Okay," Biggie said. "So, what have you found out about the body?"

The sheriff reached into his desk drawer and pulled out a plastic bag. He opened the zip lock and dumped a horn-handled knife on the desk. "Only that the knife punctured her right aorta. This here's the murder weapon." He indicated the pointed blade, which was covered with brown stains. "She must have died within minutes."

"Any prints on the knife?"

"Nothing you could use. Handle is rough, as you can see. It's a handmade knife. There's this feller out east of town got a junkyard, doncha know. He makes the things out of deer horns and old lawnmower blades. Sells um over at the hardware store. Damn good knives. I bought a couple for the wife. She swears by them."

Biggie scooted out of her chair and stood up facing the sheriff. "Well, I think I might just have to go out to the lake and interview the Baughs. And if you want my advice, Sheriff, you'll go home and go to bed. You look awful."

"I'm okay," the sheriff said. "Don't you worry about me, ma'am. But let me tell you this." He leaned across his desk and looked Biggie straight in the eye. "You had best stay away from those Baughs. You don't know those people." He sunk back down into his chair, pale and breathing hard.

Biggie walked around the desk and put her hand on the sheriff's forehead. "Deputy," she said. "I think you'd better get the sheriff home right away, and call the doctor. He seems to have a fever."

"You may be right," the sheriff said. "Wiggs, why don't you bring the car up? I think I'll go home and have a little nap."

"Good idea." Biggie turned to leave, then turned back. "By the way, Sheriff, would it be okay for the Thripps and Butch to go back to Job's Crossing? They own their own businesses and are losing money every day they stay here."

"If you'll vouch for them, Miss Biggie, of course they can leave. Just tell them I might want to call them back here if we have any more questions."

Outside on the sidewalk, Biggie looked at her watch. "Already four o'clock," she said. "I guess we'll have to wait until tomorrow to go out and interview the Baughs."

"But Biggie, the sheriff said . . ."

"Don't be silly." Biggie started off down the sidewalk. "When have you ever known me to be afraid of a bunch of redneck tough guys?"

12

When we got back to the hotel, Norman Thripp, dressed in a dorky blue jumpsuit and a gimme cap, was sitting in one of the rocking chairs out in front drinking a Diet Coke. His and Miss Mattie's suitcases was on the sidewalk beside him. "Biggie, I hope you don't mind I asked Rosebud to drive us back to Job's Crossing in your car. We'll all chip in for gas, of course."

Biggie put her hands on her hips and looked at him, then shook her head and dropped down in a chair next to him. "How did you know the sheriff was going to release you?"

"Because I know you, Biggie, and you can charm the gold out of a feller's fillings if you take the notion to."

"You're right," Biggie said. "My sakes, I'm dry as a bone." She opened up her purse and pulled out her little change purse. "J.R., go inside to the drink machine and bring me back a cold drink. A Pepsi. Get yourself one, too."

"Yes, ma'am!"

I went into the hotel lobby and down the hall, past the bar to the little alcove where the drink machines stay. Just as I was about to put the coins in, I heard the door to Miss Mary Ann's apartment slam, and Mr. Masters came out, looking real sad. He didn't see me and headed off in the direction of the kitchen muttering to himself. I got the drinks and got to the front door just as Rosebud came down the stairs wearing his chauffeur's cap.

Rosebud walked over to where Mr. Thripp was sitting. "Where's Miss Mattie and Butch?" he asked.

"They went over to the Silver Locket Gift Shoppe." Mr. Thripp stretched his long legs out in front of him. "Butch said he'd seen a blouse in there that had Mattie's name written on it, said she just *had* to go look at it. He'll probably talk her into buying a skirt and handbag to go with it." Mr. Thripp looked sad. "Oh, well, maybe it'll take her mind off my little fiasco at the gambling boats."

"Probably," Biggie said. "I can't imagine what got into you, Norman. Normally, you're tighter than wallpaper."

"I don't know, Biggie." He shook his head. "I just saw those little cherries and those money bags going around, and I guess I just lost my head. I do know one thing though, Mattie is never going to let me hear the last of this, not if I live to be a hundred. Oh, look, here they come, now."

Miss Mattie and Butch came trotting across the street. Miss Mattie had her arms full of packages and shopping bags while Butch carried a garment bag over his shoulder. They had their heads together and were giggling.

When they got to the sidewalk in front of us, Miss Mattie ran up to Biggie. "Biggie, you ought to see what I found. Butch is just a genius when it comes to shopping for clothes." She sat down on a bench and started pulling things out of the biggest bag. "Here, isn't this the cutest blouse you ever saw? And I found a darling skirt to go with it. Butch, uncover the skirt so Biggie can see."

Butch pulled up the garment bag and showed us a blue skirt with ruffles and silver trim.

"Then we went down the street to the leather shop and found boots and a purse that just match," Butch said, opening another bag. "See, robin's egg blue. That's your color, Mattie."

"I know," Miss Mattie said. "Looky here, Biggie. I even got these earrings and necklace. Genuine simulated turquoise. Aren't they perfect? See, it's a Western outfit. Won't it be wonderful to wear during rodeo week at home?"

"You'll put Dale Evans to shame," Biggie said dryly.

"Won't I? I think I'll wear it for the Founder's Day Tea in August, too," she said as she started stuffing things back in the bags. "Don't you think that would be appropriate, Biggie?" Without waiting for an answer, she turned to Mr. Thripp. "Did you finish packing, Norman?"

Mr. Thripp pointed to the suitcases lined up on the sidewalk.

"You didn't forget my toothbrush, did you? Last time we went away, you forgot to pack my toothbrush *and* my very best pair of pantyhose. I never did get them back even though I called that hotel the minute we got back. It was the time we went to Galveston for that restaurant convention. I just know some maid's wearing my pantyhose this very minute!"

Mr. Thripp unfolded himself out of the chair. "I got everything, Mattie. Can we go, now?"

Rosebud opened the trunk and started stashing the bags inside while the three others crawled into the car. Mr. Thripp up front and Miss Mattie and Butch in the back.

Rosebud turned to Biggie before he slid into the driver's seat. "I'll be back before bedtime, Miss Biggie. I don't much like leaving y'all alone in this place."

"Just be careful, and don't drive too fast," Biggie said, giving Rosebud a quick hug. "We'll be just fine."

As we were standing on the curb waving good-bye, Mr. Lew Masters came out of the hotel. "What's going on?" he asked.

"Let's go in." Biggie turned back toward the door. "It's hot out here."

I followed Biggie and Mr. Masters into the cool lobby and we all took seats on the green velvet sofas under the big Dresden chandelier.

Biggie crossed her little feet in front of her. "The Thripps and Butch are going home to take care of their businesses," she said, answering his question. "I obtained permission from the sheriff for them to leave."

"Hmm." Mr. Masters rubbed his chin. "That doesn't seem exactly fair. After all, I'm a businessman, too. Why can't I leave?"

"I'm surprised you care," Biggie said. "I should think

124

you'd be glad to stay around here and pay court to Mary Ann—or have you changed your mind about her?"

"Oh, no. Not at all." Mr. Masters crossed his legs and turned to face Biggie. "Can I confide in you, Miss Biggie?"

"Shoot."

"Well, it started three years ago. That was when they changed my territory from the Waco area to east Texas. I had heard about this little hotel from my predecessor, who always seemed to know the best places to stay while on the road."

"Umm," Biggie said.

"So, anyway, the first night I checked in here, I thought I saw an angel standing behind the desk. She was dressed all in white, and her silvery hair looked just like a halo around her head. And when she spoke, well, it was like a thousand violins."

"So, it was love at first sight." Biggie drained the last of her Pepsi and set the can on the table.

"For me, it was. Mary Ann took a lot of convincing. Been hurt in the past and all, like I told you. Anyway, I am a patient man, Miss Biggie. I plied her with gifts, flowers, candy, an occasional bottle of good wine, that sort of thing. I didn't buy anything that might be construed as too personal for fear of frightening her away. She's such a delicate creature."

"Too delicate to do murder?" Biggie murmured.

Mr. Masters looked like he had been hit in the face with cold water. "Oh, no, Miss Biggie. Surely you don't think Mary Ann . . . oh, I am shocked!"

"Never mind," Biggie said. "Go on."

Mr. Masters shook his head as if to say he couldn't

believe she had said that, then continued on. "Things were going nicely. I had even gotten her to speak of the possibility of marriage in the future. Then early this year, she changed. She gave all sorts of reasons for this change, none that seemed valid to me." He hung his head. "And now, what with this murder and all, she has sent me packing. She even says she doesn't want me staying at the hotel anymore."

"And you have no idea why?"

"Not a clue. So, Miss Biggie, if you could see your way clear to use your influence with the sheriff, I would be happy to be on my way, brokenhearted, but unbowed."

"Sorry," Biggie said. "I don't know you from Adam. The others, I can vouch for. Unless you can convince the sheriff yourself, you'll just have to stay until he releases you."

Mr. Masters nodded. "I understand," he said. "You don't know me. Oh well, what's another day or two. By the way, how is the investigation going?"

"Slowly." Biggie frowned. "Is there anything you can tell me? Anything at all?"

Mr. Masters shook his head. "Nothing . . . wait, there was one little thing, probably of no importance. I certainly didn't think so at the time . . ."

"Spit it out," Biggie said.

"Well, on the night of the murder, I'd been, well, visiting with Mary Ann until quite late in her apartment." Mr. Masters looked down at his hands then back at Biggie. "When I came out into the hall, I saw Lucas Fitzgerald come from the direction of the kitchen. He looked surprised to see me—I thought at the time it was because I was coming from, well, from Mary Ann's rooms, don't you know." He glanced sideways at me. "He started talking fast about how he couldn't sleep and had gone to the kitchen for some warm milk, but he wouldn't look me in the eye. . . ." Mr. Masters's voice trailed off.

"Interesting," Biggie said. "I wonder why he never mentioned that in his statement to the sheriff?"

"Somebody taking my name in vain?" said a voice behind me. I looked around to see Mr. Lucas Fitzgerald standing behind me. He was smiling, but I thought I saw an angry glint in his eyes. "Well, no matter. Young J.R., are you ready to go with me to the museum? I thought we'd take a little time before supper to do that work we've been talking about."

I looked at Biggie who looked hard at Lucas. "Where is this museum?" she asked.

"Only one block over and one block south." Lucas moved toward the door. "Of course, if you don't want him to go . . ."

Biggie looked at me. "I want to," I said.

As we crossed the street toward the museum, Lucas twirled his cane. "What was Masters saying about me?"

"I wasn't paying any attention," I lied.

When we climbed the steps to the big red building, I noticed a sign on the door saying that the museum was closed on Mondays.

"Don't pay any mind to that," Lucas said and pulled a ring of keys from his pocket. He put a brass key in the old-timey lock and pushed open the big door. I didn't know why, but suddenly, I felt a rabbit run over my grave as we stepped into the lobby, which was dark except for the little light that came in through the frosted glass in the door.

"Wait here," Lucas said. "I'll go ahead and turn on the lights."

I stood in the gloom for what seemed like an hour, waiting. After awhile, my eyes adjusted to the dark, and I could see the shapes of tall display cases lining a path leading to the rear of the building. I walked further into the building and looked into a room that opened to the right. I like to jumped out of my skin when I saw what I thought was a lady all dressed in old-timey clothes standing just inside the door. When I looked again, I saw it was just an old store mannequin. The rest of the room was filled with antique furniture, cases filled with old jewelry, and old portraits on the wall. I backed out of the room and waited until I saw a light come on in a room near the back. Lucas opened the door and motioned for me to come.

I followed Lucas to a huge desk covered with files and papers in the middle of a room that I thought must have been the old bank vault. The door was a foot thick and made of concrete and steel. Old lawyers' shelves with glass fronts lined the walls, and these were crammed full of files, old newspapers, and stacks of letters, some spilling over the sides. On one wall was a yellowed map of Quincy back in the old days. A hanging lamp with a green shade spread a circle of yellow light over the desk where Lucas sat. It was the only light in the room.

"Wow," I said. "I ain't . . . haven't ever seen a desk that big before."

"It's called a partner's desk," Lucas said. "One partner

sits on one side of the desk, and the other sits on the other side. See, there are drawers on both sides. This desk used to be in my daddy's law office. I donated it to the museum when I modernized my office back in '64." He motioned for me to take a seat in a swivel chair opposite him and shoved a pasteboard box toward me. "You can go through this," he said. "Put the letters in one pile, photographs in another. Anything else you find, make a new pile, which we'll call miscellaneous. Got it?"

I nodded, and went to work. I don't know why, but I just love old stuff. Always have. I was having the time of my life looking at the old pictures and reading the letters, handwritten and faded and mostly about business matters, when I noticed Lucas watching me. He smiled. "Son, you are lost in your work. You have the makings of a true historian. What do you want to be when you grow up?"

"A sportscaster on television," I said.

Lucas smiled again but didn't answer, just went back to sorting his pile of papers. We worked on for another hour before Lucas suddenly snapped his fingers. "I almost forgot something," he said. "Something I promised to show you." He got up and searched the shelves along the wall. "I know it's here somewhere," he said. "Wait! I believe it's on the top shelf. Come over here, son. I need you."

I got up and approached the shelves while Lucas opened a closet door and pulled out a stepladder. He shoved it to the shelf where he had been standing. "See that document box on the top shelf?"

"What's a document box," I asked.

"Look just next to that stack of magazines. It's black."

I climbed up the ladder and put my hand on a tin box. "This?"

"That's it. Now, hand it down to me. Careful, now."

The box was heavy, but I managed to get both hands on it and pass it down to Lucas, who put it carefully on the table. I climbed down from the ladder and stood beside him. The box had a raised top with a wire handle which had a key tied to it. Its gold decorations were so faded and worn you could barely see them. Lucas put the key into a tiny lock and raised the lid.

"This is all we have left of Diamond Lucy," he said.

"Wow," I breathed. "You said you had a picture of her."

"That's right, son. And I promised to show it to you." He removed some papers and pulled out an envelope. Out of it, he took a tiny, dark little picture. "This is a tintype," he said. "They used these before photographic paper was invented. Hold it in your hand."

The picture was heavy and cool like metal. I peered at the face. "It's hard to see."

"I know. Bring it under the lamp. If you look carefully, you will see the true face of Diamond Lucy, the most beautiful woman ever to grace our fair city."

"Prettier than Annabeth?" I asked.

Lucas smiled. "Well, son, for my money, poor little Miss Baugh was the spitting image of our own Diamond Lucy."

After staring at the picture for a few minutes, I was able to make out a face. She had blond curls and was wearing a high lace collar with a brooch pinned to it. The face, what I could see of it, was pretty, all right, but I didn't think she held a candle to Annabeth. Still, I thought, they could have been sisters. Or was I letting my imagination run away from me? I wasn't sure. I shoved the tintype back toward Lucas, who put it back into the envelope and closed the box.

Lucas was watching me. "See what I mean? Doesn't she look like the dead girl?"

"Maybe," I said. "You can't hardly tell much from that old tintype."

"Mmm," he said. "What say we work for another thirty minutes then call it a day?"

I nodded, and we went back to plowing through papers.

I was almost to the bottom of my box when I picked up a little brown leather book small enough to fit into a man's shirt pocket. I opened it and immediately lost interest when I saw it had been used to jot down expenditures. I was about to close it and put it in the miscellaneous pile when something caught my eye. *1 Jan. 1901. Augustus Baugh. $200.00.* I turned the book over and glanced at the cover. It was almost worn away, but if I held the book at a certain angle to the light, I saw engraved in gold on the front, *Elijah P. Fitzgerald, Esq.* I flipped through the pages of the book. Every month had an entry showing a payment of $200 to someone named Augustus Baugh. When I had gone through the whole book, I set it to the side of my other piles until I decided what to do. I had a feeling Biggie might be interested in seeing it, but wasn't sure how I could get it out of the museum without Lucas catching me.

I went on working on the contents of the box until I felt

eyes on me. I looked up and saw Lucas looking at me. "Son, I want you to tell me what Lew Masters was saying about me back at the hotel."

His eyes seemed to be boring a hole through me. I couldn't have lied to save my life. "Uh, not too much. Something about you getting some milk from the kitchen on the night Annabeth was killed."

Lucas nodded and went back to work. We never spoke again until he pulled out his pocket watch and announced that it was time for supper. I waited until he got up to put a stack of papers on a shelf then slipped the little ledger in my pocket.

When I got back to the hotel, Biggie was talking to Emily Faye in the lobby. I sat down to listen.

Emily Faye twisted her hands in her lap. "I didn't have any feelings about her, one way or the other."

"Honey, I have a hard time believing that," Biggie said. "I saw the way you looked at her."

"How? How did I look at her?" Emily's voice rose.

Biggie smiled. "Like you'd like to claw her eyes out. She was your rival, wasn't she?"

"Miss Biggie, I don't know what you're talking about. Why would I have to compete with some old country girl that can't even speak good English?"

"Because, honey, you're in love with Brian. Isn't that right? Tell Biggie all about it. I might even be able to help you."

Some girls can cry and it makes you feel sorry for them. You want to try and make them feel better, like—giving them a hug or something. When Emily Faye cried, you wanted to look the other way. Her eyes got all red, she snorted like a pig, and snot ran out of her nose.

Biggie dug into her purse and pulled out a handkerchief, which she put in Emily Faye's hand. Then she waited until Emily Faye stopped snorting and began hiccuping, and dabbing at her nose and eyes with the handkerchief.

Finally, Emily Faye spoke. "You're right. I do love him, but it's not going to do me one bit of good to have *her* out of the way. Brian Quincy would never look at me if I was the last girl on earth!"

"Sweetie, why do you say that? You're a pretty girl, and you could be even prettier, if you'd fix yourself up a little."

"He'll never look at me. No boy will. Miss Biggie, you just don't know . . ."

"What? What don't I know?"

Emily Faye stood up and smoothed her skirt. "I've got to go home. Mama will be expecting me." She turned toward the door.

"Oh, honey," Biggie said. "Just one more thing. Would you mind signing my little address book? Just put your name and phone number on this line here." Biggie was holding the book open in front of her.

Emily Faye wrote in the book, and went out. We watched as she ran down the sidewalk like a scalded cat.

Just as she disappeared from view, the supper bell rang. We had fried fish that Brian and his friends had caught that day at Lake O' The Pines along with slaw, potato salad, hush puppies, and Caddo Lake green tomato relish. I like the perch best. I like to bite off their little crispy tails and then strip the white meat in one piece off the backbone. I ate so many so fast that Biggie worried that I might choke on a bone.

After supper, Biggie, Lew Masters, Lucas, and Miss Mary Ann got up a game of Scrabble in the lobby. I went up to my room to play video games and forgot all about the little book in my pocket. About nine, I decided to take a nice long soak in my big claw-foot tub. The tub was deep, and I figured I could fill it with water up to my chin. While the water was running, I pulled the latest Harry Potter book out of my duffel bag and stripped off my clothes before climbing into the tub for a good read. Sure enough, the water came to my chin. I propped Harry Potter between the hot- and cold-water faucets and was soon lost in the wizard world. Biggie says I ruin all the nice books she buys because I like to read in the bathtub, but she doesn't really care because at least I'm learning to be a reader. Biggie respects people who read on account of she never does. Biggie is what you might call an *active* person. She's too busy doing things to take the time to just sit around reading. Personally, I think she's missing a lot, but I doubt whether she's going to change, her being so old and all.

I must have read for a pretty long time because all of a sudden I noticed that my water had gotten cold as pond water. I took the book off the faucets and carefully laid it down on the bathmat so I could add some more hot water, but before I could get the water turned on, I heard a soft scraping sound in the room next door. My hand froze on the faucet as I sat very still to listen, wishing Rosebud were here with me. I wasn't crazy about the idea of being all alone with a ghost in the next room. Next, I heard voices, at least I thought they must be voices, although the sounds could have been the wind whooshing through the crepe myrtle tree just outside my window. If they were voices, they spoke too low for me to understand the words. I eased myself out of the tub, being careful not to make any noise, and pulled my pants back on without even drying myself off. I tiptoed to the door and pressed my eye against the big old-fashioned keyhole. All I could see was a faint light, probably from the moon outside. The voices got louder. Now I was sure they were voices, two people, a man and a woman. I strained to listen, but the words wouldn't come clear. Then something happened that pretty near scared the wits out of me. It was the sound of a door slamming—hard. I lost my balance and fell over backward on the cold tile floor, bumping my head on the side of the tub. I sat real still, holding my head and feeling a lump rise up underneath my fingers. I was wondering if I should go and tell Biggie, when I heard another sound coming from next door. It was a woman sobbing. Sad sobs, just like the ones I'd heard that first night. Forgetting my head, I inched back to the door and tried again to look inside. Again, I couldn't see a thing. But the sobs kept on, only now their sound was growing fainter and fainter, like whoever it was was moving away from me. Finally, they faded away to—silence. I pressed my ear to the door and listened for a long time, until finally I was convinced that whoever, or whatever, it was had gone.

I stood alone in my bathroom thinking. Should I go for Rosebud? No, I couldn't do that because Rosebud had gone to take the others back to Job's Crossing. So I asked myself what Rosebud would do if he were in my shoes, and the answer came immediately. Rosebud would go and investigate. But Rosebud was a man, and strong; I was just a kid. Just then, my eye fell on a long-handled plunger near the wall behind the toilet. I picked it up and, pretending it was Harry Potter's wand, I slowly turned the dead bolt, flinching when it clicked, and inched the door open. I stood for a moment inside the room until my eyes adjusted to the dark, then took a few steps inside. The room was completely quiet and, I could feel it, it was completely empty as well. Gripping my plunger, I tiptoed to the side wall and flipped on the light switch. The room was just as it had been. The high canopy bed stood out from the wall facing me. French doors with lacy curtains opened onto the balcony, just as they did in our room. An old-style marble-topped dresser with a tall mirror was set at an angle in the corner and, along the wall next to the hall, the tall wardrobe still stood. It was the same, but different. I scanned the room again and my eyes lit on the wardrobe. That was it. The doors to the wardrobe were ajar. I walked over to take a peep inside, expecting to find it full of old clothes, or maybe boxes. Instead, it was completely empty. I was about to close the doors when my eye fell on something strange. Inside the wardrobe I saw a footprint in the dust, small, like a lady or a kid. When I bent over to get a better look, I spotted a square door in the bottom of that wardrobe, exactly like the one Biggie has to get into her attic. In the middle of the door was a hole just big enough for one finger.

Now what? I thought. Should I try to open that door with my finger? What if I did and a ghost was down there just waiting to come whooshing up into my face? Or, worse, what if the murderer was hiding down there? What would Biggie do? Then I had my answer. Biggie wasn't afraid of any old ghost. Biggie wasn't afraid of anything.

I put my finger in the hole and was surprised at how easily the door lifted up. A blast of cold air came up out of the darkness and slapped me in the face. No ghost, just cold air. Suddenly, I remembered the cold spot I had noticed the first time I'd been in this room.

I stepped into the wardrobe, being careful not to disturb the footprint, and peered down into the hole. I could see steps going down. Wishing I had a flashlight, I slowly put one foot on the first step. I looked down into total blackness. I stepped back out of the wardrobe. No way I'm going down there, I thought. Then I remembered something. I stepped back out of the wardrobe and went back through the bathroom to my bedroom. I looked on the old washstand that held my television. Sure enough, there was the little scented votive candle and next to it, the china ashtray with its book of matches still unused. The candle was small and wouldn't give out much light, but it would have to do.

I picked up the tee shirt I'd worn that day and pulled it over my head and put on my shoes without socks. I took the candle and matches and started back to the wardrobe. I got as far as the bathroom before I lost my nerve. I put the lid down on the toilet thinking I'd just sit down a minute to calm myself. Leaning back, I closed my eyes and tried to think brave thoughts. I thought of my friend, Monica, who is the bravest person I know outside of Biggie and Rosebud.

My mind went back to one day last summer when Monica had decided to show me a cave she'd discovered down on the banks of Wooten Creek.

"It's the scariest place I've ever seen," she said. "I 'spect you'll be too chicken to go in there, J.R."

We were stepping high through the tall grass in Monica's daddy's pasture. Monica's dog, Buster, was running ahead with his nose to the ground.

"Me?" I said. "Me, scared? You must have me mixed up with somebody else. I'm not scared of any old cave."

"Well, you better be scared of this one," she said. "On account of they tell that a really mean black man named Amos Durley's got a still in there and if he finds anybody messing with it, he cuts them up in little pieces and uses their bodies for catfish bait." Monica climbed through a bob wire fence then held the wires up for me to crawl through.

After that, we cut through the woods until we came to the banks of the creek. Monica pointed to the opposite bank. "See that clump of sumac?"

I nodded.

"It's behind that. Come on!"

I looked at the sky. The sun was getting low. "It's getting late. You reckon we ought to wait until tomorrow?"

"Naw. Come on." Monica was already walking across a sandbar in the creek. "Follow me, and you won't get your feet wet."

Buster swam across and was already rooting around in the sumac bushes when we got there. Suddenly, there was a rustling noise, and three armadillos came scuttling out of the bushes. I like to jumped out of my skin.

Naturally, Monica laughed her head off. "Come on," she said. "A little old armadillo can't hurt you."

"I know it," I said, miffed.

I followed Monica until we came to the entrance of the cave. The air coming out felt cool but smelled to high heaven."

"Pee-yew!" I said.

Monica turned around and grinned at me.

We hadn't gotten far into the cave when Buster came trotting back out with something in his mouth.

"What's that?" I asked.

"Oh, Buster's probably caught a mole. Ain't he smart?"

I didn't answer, because I don't have as high an opinion of Buster as Monica does.

Now, we turned a corner and suddenly it was pitch-black in the cave. The smell was getting worse. "Okay," Monica said. "Now, let's just set down and rest. In a minute, you're going to get the surprise of your life."

"Probably Amos Durley coming to cut us up into fish bait," I said. But I sat down on a rock next to Monica. "I don't know why you got the bright idea to show me this old cave anyway. We could be fishing."

"Just wait," Monica said.

It wasn't long before I knew what she meant. At first it was just a faint rustling sound. Then I began to hear some tweeting noises. "Birds?" I asked.

Monica grabbed my arm. "Just sit still and be quiet."

I tried, but seconds later, I felt something soft brush the top of my head.

"What was that?" I started to stand up, but Monica held me back.

"Now, duck!" she said.

I put my head between my knees just before I felt a rush of air as thousands of tiny wings fluttered over our heads and the tweeting sound became a roar. Bats! Monica had brought me to a bat cave.

"Keep your head down," she said, giggling, "if you don't want to get a face full of bat poop. Ain't this fun?"

"Yeah, fun," I said, covering my head with my hands.

After what seemed like a long time but was probably just a few minutes, the sounds stopped. Monica grabbed my hand and pulled me toward the mouth of the cave. "Look!" she shouted, pointing to the sky.

What looked like a cigar-shaped black cloud was shooting toward the setting sun. Bats, thousands of them, were flying off for a night of hunting bugs.

Sitting on that toilet in the hotel, I suddenly saw Monica's face in front of me, laughing and calling me chicken because I was too scared to investigate a little trap door. I got up and started toward the wardrobe room.

13

An hour later, I was standing in the hall pounding on Biggie's door as loud as I could.

Biggie, wearing her little short-tailed nightie, opened the door a crack and peered out, then swung it open as soon as she saw it was me. "Honey, what's the matter? You look like you've seen a ghost!" She pulled me into the room.

I stood just inside her door panting on account of I'd run all the way back upstairs.

"J.R., are you all right?" Biggie put her hands on my shoulders and looked me in the eye.

"Yes'm," I said, "but I found out something really important, Biggie." I flopped down on her bed and started in telling her all about the voices in the next room and about the little door in the bottom of the wardrobe.

"My soul." Biggie, who had climbed back in bed and

141

wrapped the covers around her knees, leaned forward. "Did you look down there?"

"Better'n that. I *went* down there. See, Biggie, there were these stairs leading down. Oo-wee, was it dark! But I'd taken a candle, see, so I could see just a little bit. The steps led down a pretty long way and, Biggie, there were spiders as big as your hand in there."

"Did you see one?" Biggie asked, and I thought I saw a twinkle in her eye.

"Um, I didn't exactly what you'd call *see* one, but I saw their webs—and they were huge!"

"Okay," Biggie said, "go on."

"Well, when I came to the end of the stairs, I came to this, like room thing, you know?"

Biggie nodded.

"And it was like a cellar, or something, dirt floor and brick walls, all musty and kind of damp."

"Was anything in there?" Biggie poured a glass of water from the pitcher by her bed and took a sip, then handed it to me.

I drank some water and went on. "Yes'm, but that comes later. See, it was pitch dark in there except for my candle which was about to go out and a little square of light that was coming in from one wall. I walked over to that light and, guess what, it was the same little door me and Rosebud had found out in the courtyard. Remember, Biggie? Where we found Annabeth's purse?"

"I remember."

"So, anyway, I went over and pushed open the little door (It ain't—isn't—much taller than I am.) and poked my head out to make sure there wasn't anybody hanging around out in the courtyard. When I saw the coast was clear, I left the door open so I could see a little better by the moonlight."

"J.R., you're getting as windy as Rosebud. Just tell me what you found."

"It had some benches around the sides, wide so somebody could sleep on um, and a few old bottles and jars scattered around on the floor. A pile of old rags or clothes was in the corner, but I wasn't about to touch that mess. It most likely would have had a rat's nest in it."

"So, then what did you do?"

"Came back to my room. By then, my candle was really getting low, so I just closed the little door and skedaddled back up the stairs. Whatcha think, Biggie?"

Biggie squinted her eyes and looked at the ceiling. "I think maybe you have just discovered the abolitionist's secret."

"Huh?"

"Hosiah Tilley," Biggie said. "Remember at lunch Saturday, Lucas was telling us that an abolitionist used to own this hotel, and he helped runaway slaves escape?"

"Oh, yeah. And they said he had a secret place here in the hotel where he hid them."

"Right," Biggie said. "He'd hide them in that little room you found, then at night, he'd take them out, give them a horse from the livery stable next door and a twenty-dollar gold piece and send them on their way. But there's more. J.R., tell me again about the ghost you saw on the night Annabeth was killed."

I paused a minute, remembering. "Well, I was in the bathroom, just like tonight, and I heard somebody crying, real faint. I opened the door and felt a cold wind brush past me. Biggie! They must have opened the trapdoor and got away just as I came in there. That's what that cold wind was. It wasn't a ghost at all!" I breathed a sigh of relief. "Biggie, I'll bet that was Annabeth crying that night." Then I thought of something. "But who was crying in there tonight? Biggie, do you reckon it was Annabeth's ghost?"

"No, I don't," Biggie said. "I reckon it was a flesh-and-blood person. And I reckon we're going to find out who it was. What's that sticking out of your pocket?"

I pulled the little book out and handed it to Biggie. "I stole it from the museum, but don't be mad, Biggie. I thought you ought to see it."

Biggie flipped through the book.

"I'll show you." I crawled up beside Biggie and turned the pages to the first entry about Augustus Baugh. "They're all the way through the book, Biggie. Lucas's granddaddy was paying money to Annabeth's family. Didn't you want to see that?"

"You did the right thing," Biggie said. "Now, let's get some sleep. Do you want to spend the night in here with me?"

"Uh-uh. What are you going to do next, Biggie?"

"I'm not right sure, but eventually, we're going to have to go out to Caddo Lake and interview the Baughs. Now, scoot off to bed."

The next day was Tuesday. We had already been at this hotel five days, and I don't mind telling you, I was past ready to go home. I woke early and hurried down to the kitchen to talk to Willie Mae and Rosebud. Willie Mae was pouring batter into muffin cups.

"What's that?" I asked sliding into a kitchen chair.

"Cranberry walnut muffins," Willie Mae said. "They be ready in fifteen minutes. Get you some milk out of the icebox."

"I'd rather have coffee," I said.

"You know coffee'll stunt your growth, and you ain't no bigger than a flea right now." Willie Mae slid the muffin pan into the oven.

"Can I have eggs?"

Willie Mae sighed and took a frying pan from the pot rack over the stove. "How you want um cooked?"

"Eyeballs," I said.

Willie Mae put a glob of butter in the pan and stirred it around with the spatula until it was melted. Rosebud came into the room and stood beside her as she cracked two eggs into the butter.

"Best put three more in there," he said. "I'm hungry as a hog this morning. Boy, them folks were sure glad to get back home. They jabbered my head off all the way."

Willie Mae dropped three more eggs into the pan. "You sure took your good time getting back."

"I reckon I was glad to be there, too," Rosebud said. "I brought in the mail and swept the leaves off the front porch before I come on back."

Willie Mae looked over her shoulder at me. "If you want any toast, you better put you some bread in the toaster. I ain't got but two hands."

"Rosebud," I said, dropping two slices of bread into

the toaster, "how old were you when you started drinking coffee?"

"Six," he said.

Willie Mae gave him a look.

"Sixteen, I meant." He winked at me. "I was sixteen before I ever laid a lip around a coffee mug."

I decided to let the matter drop. "Who's taking care of Booger and Bingo while we're gone?"

Willie Mae put two fried eggs on my plate and three on Rosebud's. "Miz Moody taken the puppy to her house to stay. I left plenty of food and water for that cat out on the back porch."

"Old Booger was layin' up on the porch rail purrin' his head off when I left," Rosebud said.

"I'm about ready to go home," I said, spearing an egg yolk with a piece of toast.

Just then, Biggie came bustling into the kitchen. She was dressed to go out. "My soul, I slept too late," she said. "This morning, I want to go down to the courthouse. I have a feeling we might find some answers to why Judge Fitzgerald was making payments to Augustus Baugh somewhere in the county records." She poured herself a cup of coffee and took a seat at the table.

"Biggie, I was just saying that I'm about ready to go home."

"I am, too," she said. "And we will just as soon as we find out who murdered poor Annabeth. Come to the court-house and help me run the records."

When we got to the county clerk's office, who should be standing behind the counter than Emily Faye LaRue.

"Why, Emily," Biggie said, "I didn't know you worked here."

"I just work mornings," Emily said, not looking Biggie in the eye. "I took over from Jen Meeks. She's just had a baby."

"Are you going to college this fall?"

"I don't guess so."

"Why?"

"Mama doesn't think it's necessary. I guess I'd like to."

"We'll talk later," Biggie said. "Right now, I want to look at all the records from 1900 to around 1920. Birth, marriage, death certificates, deeds, the works."

The walls behind the tall counter were lined with file cabinets, and I could see an open door behind her that led to another room filled with tall shelves holding the big books of deeds and stuff.

Emily pulled a pad toward her and wrote down the dates. She went into a little side office marked COUNTY CLERK and spoke to someone, then came back carrying a key. "Those records are downstairs in the basement," she said. "I can take you down there—or, if you'd rather, you can look at them on microfilm here in this office."

"I want to see the originals," Biggie said.

Emily led us down the hall to a flight of marble steps that led into the basement. She turned right and pretty soon we came face-to-face with another thick door like the one I'd seen at the museum. "We keep them in this vault," she said, inserting her key and turning the big wheel that opened the door. Emily flipped on a light and commenced to show Biggie where the different records were kept.

When she was through, Biggie watched while she left the room and then began pulling books off the shelves.

"You take the deeds," she said. "Mark everything that has the name of Baugh or Fitzgerald. The judge may have bought a piece of land from Augustus Baugh. On second thought, check the notary's signature down at the bottom of the documents. Back in the old days, attorneys used to notarize their own work. It's possible the judge was making those payments for someone else. I'll run the marriage, birth, and death records."

We worked along in silence for a long time. All of the deeds were written by hand, and the language they used was funny. I was barely halfway through 1882 when Biggie slapped the page she was looking at.

"Well, I'll be," she said. "This might be our answer. A birth certificate. It says on January 1, 1900, a baby girl, Marcella, was born to Rachel Quincy. Funny, they don't give a father's name."

"I reckon she wasn't married."

"I guess. But that's not all. On that same date, a child, stillborn, was born to one Augustus Baugh and his wife, Coralee. J.R., leave the deed records and start looking through probate. Find every will that was filed in the name of Quincy and see if the name Marcella shows up."

That took a while. Plenty of Quincys died, but none had an heir named Marcella. I shoved that aside and started looking through marriages. "Biggie, here's something funny," I said.

"Hmm?" Biggie had her head in the death certificates.

"Biggie, it says here, a lady named Marcella Baugh got married to Ralph Meeks in December of 1914."

"Let me see that," Biggie said. "Well, if it is the same child, she got married at fourteen. But I don't suppose that was unheard of back then—especially among country folks. Run upstairs and ask Emily if we can get copies of these papers, the two birth certificates and the marriage license."

I came back to tell her Emily says we can have the copies, but she'll have to make them from the microfilm. The books can't leave this room. She says get the volume and page for her, and she'll make the copies.

It was lunchtime by the time we got back to the hotel. Biggie had the copies in her big black purse.

"Who can tell me how to get to the Baugh place?" Biggie asked when we were all seated at the big table in the dining room.

Miss Mary Ann set a plate of cornbread on the corner of the table and looked at Biggie. "Biggie, I don't think . . . I mean . . . do you really think you should go out there? Those people . . ."

"I really don't advise it, Miss Biggie." Lew Masters looked serious.

"Rosebud is driving us." Biggie spooned butterbeans with little bits of ham onto her plate.

"You take Highway 18 out of town going east." Lucas smeared butter on a piece of cornbread, being careful to get it all over. "When you see a sign pointing to Nowhere, turn right. Keep going until you come to Beck's Bait Shop. They'll be able to tell you where to go from there."

"Nowhere?" I said.

"It's the name of a town, and when you get there, you'll see why," Brian said.

149

"Have you ever been there?"

"A few times." Brian looked down at his plate.

Rosebud drove the car to the outskirts of town and turned east on Highway 18. We passed pretty little farms and ranches with white houses and red barns and mowed pastures. Occasionally we would see a great big house sitting back on a hill. Biggie said those were most likely owned by Dallas folks who had come to the country to retire.

"Why Dallas folks?" I asked.

"Because the locals who could afford houses like that wouldn't move this far out in the country on a bet," Biggie said.

"How come?"

"Oh, J.R., they just wouldn't. Don't ask so many questions."

A few miles farther out, the farms got shabbier, with fences falling and unpainted barns with tin roofs. After a while, the pine trees grew thicker and closer to the road, and the farms disappeared altogether. Every now and then we'd pass an acre or two that looked like a tornado had come through leaving just a few scrawny trees behind. Rosebud said those were places where the timber had been cut.

"It's ugly," I said.

"Those trees were planted for cutting," Biggie said. "There's very little virgin timber left in these parts. However, you'll see some around the lake. That's protected land."

"Rosebud," I said, just to make conversation so Biggie wouldn't launch into her conservation lecture, which I'd heard about a million times, "do you like living with us?"

"Sure."

"Better than anyplace you've ever lived before?"

"I'd say just about." Rosebud looked over his shoulder at me and grinned.

"Well, what if you won the lottery and could live anyplace in the world. Where would you live then?"

"Nowhere," Rosebud said.

"Huh? Rosebud, you can't . . ."

"Nowhere." Rosebud pointed ahead. "There's the sign." He turned left onto a one-lane gravel road. "I reckon this here must be the bait shop."

Rosebud pulled the car into a bumpy drive and parked beside a gas pump in front of a rickety building. A homemade sign on the top said BECK'S BAIT SHOP AND BAR. A wooden box on legs stood under the grimy front window. WORMS was spray painted in black across the front of the box. The screen door opened and slammed behind a man with a big beer belly. He was wearing overalls over a grubby tee shirt and running shoes with no laces or socks. The edges of his lips were stained with tobacco juice. He looked at Biggie's big car.

"You folks get lost from the rest of the funeral?" He grinned a big toothless grin.

Biggie jumped out of the car and trotted up to the man. "Nope," she said. "Just need a tank full of gas and a little information."

The man took the nozzle from the pump and stuck it in

the fuel tank. While the gas pumped, Rosebud asked the man how to get to the Baugh place.

"Ya'll ain't the laws, is you?" The man looked first at Biggie, then Rosebud, then me.

"Do we look like law enforcement officers?" Biggie shot back.

"No'm. Reckon not."

"Biggie, I could use a Big Red," I said.

"Good idea," Biggie said, pulling a bill out of her purse. Go in and get us all a cold drink."

"Go on in the back and tell Marge to give you what you want," the man said.

The screen door drug the floor, and I had to lift it up to get it open. I stepped into a dingy room with a counter running along the back wall and shelves all around which held cans of Copenhagen and Skoll snuff, cigarettes, motor oil, sardines, Vienna sausages, crackers, and a few jars of peanut butter. An old-timey Coke box, the kind you open from the top, stood in one corner with a sign over it that said, BAIT SHRIMP—$2.00, LIVER—50 CENTS A POUND, MINNOWS OUT BACK. I opened the lid and peeked in. It smelled to high heaven.

I looked up and noticed a door to the left of the counter, which was open. The sign above it said BAR–BILLIARDS. I heard George Strait singing about Amarillo by morning. I poked my head in the room, which was only lit by a jukebox and a couple of beer signs over the bar. A fat man was feeding coins into a pinball machine.

"Can I hep yew?" said a voice from the darkness.

Feeling really grown-up, I walked up to the bar and sat down on a stool. I slapped the five Biggie had given me down and said, "I'll have a Diet Coke, an R.C., and a Big Red."

While a big woman with half-black and half-blond hair was getting the drinks, I had a look around. At a table in the corner by the jukebox, four teenage boys and one girl were drinking beer and talking real loud. When a slow dance started playing, the girl and one of the boys got up to dance. The girl was wearing a bikini top and really short cutoffs. The boy had his hands all over her, which was pretty sickening if you ask me. The girl didn't seem to mind, though. She had herself plastered against him so tight you couldn't have gotten a dollar bill between the two of them. They were moving pretty slow, but finally he turned her around. She looked at me and I like to have fell off that bar stool. It was none other than Emily LaRue. I think she recognized me because she hid her face in the boy's neck and wouldn't look back at me again.

Quick as I could, I grabbed my drinks and change and hurried on out of there to tell Biggie what I'd seen. They were already sitting in the car, and before I could get a word out, Rosebud had pulled out of the driveway and we were sailing down the road.

"Are you positive it was Emily?" Biggie asked.

"Yes'm."

Biggie turned and faced me. "And she was dressed how?"

"I told you, Biggie. She didn't have hardly anything on. And she was acting real rude."

"Rude? How?"

I don't like to talk about such things in front of Biggie. "You remember that movie, *Dirty Dancing*?"

Biggie nodded.

"Well, that's what they were doing, dirty dancing—only they weren't as good as that couple in the movie."

Biggie grinned. "Rosebud, turn this car around. I've got to go see this for myself."

So, Rosebud turned the car around and Biggie went in and peeked into the bar then came back out shaking her head. "Let's go," was all she said.

14

The Baugh house sat in a clearing in the pines at the end of a rutty dirt road. It was a big house, unpainted, built up on stilts with a porch around the front and sides. Four skinny old cow dogs ran out from under the porch wagging their tails and sniffing us. I think they were hoping we had some food on us. Rosebud tossed them the peanut butter crackers he'd bought at the store, and the dogs swallowed them down and commenced whining for more.

"Go on, dogs," Rosebud said. "Miss Biggie, y'all stay here while I see if anybody's home."

He climbed up the steps to the porch and knocked on the door. A tall man came out followed by an even taller woman who had dyed black hair slicked back in a bun. After her, came two boys who looked to be about Brian's age wearing overalls with no shirts. Rosebud spoke to them for a minute and then motioned for us to come.

Biggie walked up to the man, stuck out her little hand and said, "Good afternoon, Mr. Baugh. I'm Biggie Weatherford from over in Job's Crossing. This is my grandson, J.R., and my associate, Rosebud Robichaux.

The man looked at Biggie like she'd lost every one of her marbles while the two boys scratched themselves. Finally, the woman spoke up. "Well'm this here's my husband, Mule." She pointed to the two boys. "Them's the twins, Travis and Crockett. My name's Faye. Now, what 'chall want with us?"

Biggie explained about how we had been at the hotel when Annabeth was killed. "It was a terrible thing," she said, "and I intend to find out who did it. Could you spare us a few minutes of your time?"

The man's bushy brows came together and he glared at Biggie. "Ain't you a town woman?"

Biggie nodded.

"Git!" he said.

Biggie turned to the woman. "She was a beautiful child with her whole life ahead of her. You're her mother. Don't you want to know who did this to her?"

"Git!" the man said, louder this time.

"Shut up, Mule." The woman seemed to tower over her husband. "It ain't no sense in you gittin' your guts in a uproar. It don't cost nothin' to hear what she's got to say." She turned to Biggie. "Come on in and set a minute."

While the adults went inside to talk, I spied an old tire swing hanging from the limb of a chinaberry tree. Since I don't get many chances to ride in a tire swing (Biggie won't have one in her yard), I decided to try it out. I was

156

busy going around and around to twist the rope up real good so that when I let go, I'd whirl around in circles, when I heard a sound behind me, something like a giggle, but not exactly like one.

I let the swing unwind slowly, keeping my toe on the ground, for one time around so I could look to see what had made the sound. All I saw was the house, a barn, an old wagon, and some cows grazing behind a slat-rail fence. Must have been a bird, I thought, and lifted my toe off the ground to let the swing spin around and around as the rope unwound itself. When it finally stopped, I was dizzy, and, as the world spun around me, I saw something that hadn't been there before. It was a person, or I thought it must have been a person, because it was standing on two legs. But that's where the resemblance stopped. This creature had a mess of black hair sticking out in all directions. It was dressed in what looked like a potato sack with holes cut for arms, no shoes, and its arms and legs were brown and covered with scratches and mosquito bites. It was definitely laughing at me.

"What's so funny?" I don't like to be laughed at.

The creature pointed at me.

"Huh!" I said. "You ain't much to be makin' fun of anybody."

It must have thought that was a real funny joke, because it laughed so hard it had to bend over, holding its sides.

"I don't have to take this," I said. "I'm going to the house." I pulled my legs out of the swing and turned away.

"Wait! Don't go." The voice was like music. I spun

around and stared. Suddenly, I noticed the eyes. They were sky blue, almost too light to belong to a human, more like the eyes of a kitten.

"Where 'bouts did you come from?"

"Over yonder." It pointed toward the barnyard.

"Do you always go around scaring people?"

Another giggle.

I squinted at it. "What are you, anyway, a boy, or a girl?"

Before you could say "Jack Robinson" it lifted up the potato sack, and I could see right away that it was a girl.

"Don't be doin' that," I said, embarrassed. "You live up there?" I pointed toward the house.

"Tee-hee-hee."

"Well, what's so all-fired funny?"

"Me, livin' in the big house."

"What's so funny about that? Hey, are you crazy or something?"

"I live over yonder in the hen house." The girl pointed toward the chicken house, which was leaning so bad it looked like a strong wind would blow it over, and had inch-deep cracks between the boards.

"You what?"

She looked at me like I was the one that was weird. "I live in the hen house. Got me an old bed in there an' everything. Him and her, they don't never let me in the house."

I looked at the girl. Dirty and ragged as she was, there was something familiar about her. The hair was black, and the nose was different, but she had the same pale blue eyes and slender figure that Annabeth had had.

"Hey," I said. "Was Annabeth your sister?"

I like to jumped out of my skin when she commenced howling like a coyote, tears streaming out of her eyes and making rivers in the dirt that covered her face. "Her's gone," she said. "Her gone away and left myself alone." She howled some more.

"Hush up," I said. "You're liable to disturb them up at the house."

She hushed right away and looked up at the house like she was scared to death. "Them better not come." She took a step back toward the barnyard.

"Wait, don't go. You got a name?"

She stopped, still watching the house. "Uh-huh."

"Well, what is it?"

"Loosie-Goosie." She swiped at her face with one grubby hand, leaving a trail of dirt across her cheek.

"That ain't a name. What's your real name?"

"Loosie-Goosie's all I know. Hey, you ever see a alligator?"

"In the zoo's all."

"Want to see one? I know where's a whole bunch of um."

I looked up at the house. "I don't know. We've got to be going pretty soon. Is it far?"

"See through them trees?" She pointed toward the back of the house.

I nodded.

"Lake's right there. I got a boat down there."

I figured this might be my only chance to get a look at Caddo Lake so, against my better judgment, I followed her.

"Keep your head down," she said as we rounded the side of the house. "Don't let um see us."

We climbed under a bob-wire fence and started across an overgrown field. Pretty quick, I realized that those trees were farther off than they had looked at first. Loosie-Goosie walked barefooted right through a clump of bull nettles. I stepped around it, being careful not to let the nettles touch my skin. Finally, we reached the trees and I looked back toward the house, now just barely visible through the trees.

"Come on!" she yelled, darting in and out among the pines and sweetgums. Now the ground started to get marshy, and I could smell the lake. "Here!" she shouted.

By the time I caught up with her, she was untying a rope tied around an oak sapling, that was attached to a flat-bottomed boat. I stopped and looked around me. This lake was not one bit like our lake at home, which is open and blue. This lake was dark and spooky, the water almost black in the shade. Cypress trees draped with Spanish moss grew along the edges and out into the black water, their roots gnarled and wide at the bottom. The whole lake, as far as I could see, was a forest of trees with branches that hung so low some grazed the water.

"Well, git in." She was already seated in the back of the boat, holding a long-handled paddle.

I got in.

"Don't you have any oars?"

"*Oars, oars, got no oars. Got some whores and lots of boars, but I ain't got no oars,*" she sang. "What's oars?"

"Never mind," I said, wondering what had possessed me to come here with her. She was obviously nutty as a squirrel, but it was too late to change my mind; she was already pushing the boat away from shore with that funny long paddle.

I looked around as we drifted through what seemed to be a broad channel that wound like a watery road through the trees. A great white heron swooped down near the shore and waded through the murky water, occasionally dunking his head and coming up with a fish in his beak. I liked to jumped out of my skin as a fat, black water moccasin swam by making a vee in the water not two feet from the boat.

"How far to the alligators?" I asked, and I'll admit, my voice might have been just a little bit shaky.

"*Alligator, crocodile, maybe a minute, maybe a mile.*"

Now, I was nervous. I looked behind me, but all I could see was a wall of trees. It was getting darker as the trees grew thicker, and the branches almost covered the sky.

"Let's go back," I said, hoping she didn't notice the tremor in my voice. "There's not any alligators around here."

Loosie-Goosie dug the paddle into the mud of the lake bottom, stopping the boat. "Look," she whispered. We had drifted to a place where a point of land jutted out into the water.

At first, I didn't see anything but buckeye shrubs, cattails, and a few logs half submerged in the water. Then, one of those logs moved, then another and another. Loosie-Goosie sat very still in the boat, a little smile on her face. I looked closer and saw a partially submerged head with two round searching eyes. Alligators! Huge ones! I stared, afraid to move, while one opened his mouth wide

161

showing off two rows of sharp yellow teeth. "I see four of them," I breathed.

"*One, two, three, four. That's all there is, there ain't no more,*" she sang softly.

One of the gators slowly turned himself in the water so that one of his ugly eyes stared straight at our boat.

"Shhh," I hissed. Suddenly, I realized that I'd made a big mistake. I should never have let this crazy girl talk me into coming with her. "Let's go back," I whispered.

"The little titty-baby wants to go back," she said, almost to herself. "Us just rock the baby to sleep. That's what us'll do; us'll rock the baby." With that, she put her hands on either side of the boat and commenced rocking from side to side. "*Go to sleepy, little baby. Go to sleepy, little baby,*" she sang, rocking harder and harder until the sides of the boat slapped the water with each rock.

"*Go to sleepy, little baby.*" Slap, Slap. "*Go to sleepy, little baby.*" Slap.

I tried to hold on, but the water was making the edges of the boat slippery. I tried to grab the wooden plank I was sitting on, but it came loose from the boat and flew out of my hands. I grabbed wildly for anything to hold on to just before I toppled over the side. Just as my face hit the water, I thought I heard Biggie calling, "J.R.! J.R.!"

The next thing I remember is bumping down the road away from the Baugh's place sitting in the backseat of Biggie's car. I was wrapped in an old camp blanket Rosebud keeps in the trunk. My hair was caked with mud; my head hurt; my ears were stopped up and rattled whenever I turned my head. I smelled like mud and dead fish. The wool blanket itched and stuck to my skin.

"At least, I'm not dead," I said.

"You might have been." Biggie turned around in the seat and glared at me. "What in the world were you thinking about, J.R. Don't you have a brain in your head?"

I didn't think she expected an answer.

Rosebud was wearing the army green coveralls he keeps in the back of the car for fishing. "I ought to whup your butt," he said. This was serious. Rosebud was never mad at me.

"I'm sorry." I squirmed under the itchy blanket. "How'd I get rescued?"

"We couldn't find you when we got ready to go," Biggie said. "I called and called. Finally, Mrs. Baugh said maybe you'd gone to the lake. When we got there and saw the boat gone, we went around the shoreline looking and calling."

"We were way, far out," I said.

"Not as far as you thought." Rosebud drove slow around a pothole. "There's a trail that goes around the lake. Took us right to where y'all was." He shook his head. "When you fell out of the boat, you hit your head on the side. Knocked you clean out."

"What happened to that crazy girl, Loosie-Goosie? I'd like to kill her."

"Her pa just about did," Rosebud said. "Started right in beatin' her upside the head with the boat paddle. I had to pull him off of her."

I felt sick to my stomach. "And y'all just left her there?"

"I'm going straight to child protective the minute we get back to town," Biggie said.

"They make her live in the hen house," I said, starting to feel just a little bit sorry for her.

"We'll soon put a stop to that," Biggie said. "She'll be taken out of that home and put in foster care."

"This blanket itches," I whined.

"You stink, too," Biggie said. "Rosebud, let's stop somewhere and get J.R. cleaned up. Look, there's a house right up there, and somebody's outside. Maybe they'll let us clean him up with their hose."

"Yeah," I said. "And, Biggie, I just remembered, I left my gym bag in the trunk when school let out last May. I got some clothes in there."

Rosebud pulled the car into the driveway in front of a little white house that was set close to the road. The yard was clipped neat as a pin, and I could see tubs of red geraniums growing on each side of the front door. An old black man was standing out in the yard watching a little dog do its business.

Biggie jumped out of the car and walked up to the man, who took off his old felt hat and smiled at her. She spoke to him for a minute and pointed to me. He nodded his head and she motioned for us to come.

"This is Mr. Hance Johnson," she said. "He doesn't have a hose, but there's a well out back with a bucket."

"Pleased to meet you," Mr. Johnson said. "Looks like y'all had a little accident." He pronounced it *acci-DENT*.

"I just about got eaten by some alligators." I couldn't wait to get back to Job's Crossing and tell Monica about my close call. She'd never believe it.

164

"We were visiting with the Baughs. Their daughter took J.R. out in a boat, then tipped him over into the lake."

"Mmmm." Mr. Johnson was watching his dog. "That girl tetched. Uh-hmm."

"Do you know much about that family?"

"I mostly don't go 'round them, lest I cain't hep it." Mr. Johnson kept on looking at his dog.

"Rosebud," Biggie said, "why don't you take J.R. around back and help him clean up while I talk to Mr. Johnson."

Rosebud opened the trunk and got out my gym bag, and we went around to the back of the house. Up close to the tiny screened-in porch was a well with a bucket and rope hanging over it.

"Strip," Rosebud said.

I looked around. There wasn't even a tree to hide behind. "Here?"

"You betcha." Rosebud was already lowering the bucket into the well.

I figured I was already in enough trouble, so I stripped and stood there, shivering, while Rosebud poured bucket after bucket of icy-cold water over me. He opened my gym bag and pulled out a towel, tossing it to me. Fast as I could, I dried myself off and put on my shorts and tee shirt.

"Rosebud, are you still mad at me?"

"You did a dern-fool thing and mighty near got me and you both killed," Rosebud said. "Ain't I got a right to be mad?"

"I guess. Rosebud, did you pull me out?"

"Who else?"

"Thanks," I said, following him back to the car and thinking how Rosebud was the best friend I had in the world and I had almost gotten him eaten by an alligator. I'd have to think of something real good to make it up to him.

Me and Rosebud got back in the car and waited while Biggie finished talking to Mr. Johnson. He was doing most of the talking, all the while pointing back toward the Baugh place. Every once in a while, Biggie would ask a question and he would talk some more. Finally, she came back to the car and slid into her seat. She waved to Mr. Johnson.

"What all were y'all talking about, Biggie?" I asked.

"You'll find out soon enough." Biggie looked out the window and wouldn't say another word. I hate it when she does that.

15

When we got back to the hotel, a familiar smell made my mouth water. "Fried chicken!" I yelled and headed toward the kitchen.

"Not so fast." Biggie caught me by the elastic waistband of my gym shorts. "Upstairs with you, first. Get a good bath, shampoo your hair, and get into some clean clothes. Then you can sit down for supper like a gentleman."

I got cleaned up in no time on account of I was having a fit to get downstairs and get my lips around some of Willie Mae's good fried chicken. It's my favorite thing in the whole world. The others were all seated at the table when I slid into my place. Biggie took her napkin and wiped a little soap I had missed from behind my ear. "My soul," she said. "You must be hungry."

"I guess you would be, too, if you'd almost gotten

eaten alive by an alligator." I looked at the platter of chicken that was being passed around the table, hoping nobody would get the pulley bone before it got to me.

"Don't be a smart aleck." Biggie spooned a pile of mashed potatoes onto her plate and slopped some cream gravy on top. "Want some potatoes?"

I nodded, then looked around the table because everything had suddenly gotten quiet. The people had all stopped eating and were staring at me.

"What?" I said.

"Well, land's sakes, J.R.," Miss Mary Ann said. "You just said you almost got eaten by an alligator!"

"What happened?" Mr. Lew Masters looked at me, concerned.

Brian, who was sitting on my left, mussed my hair. "Like, what happened, man?"

So I told them. I left out the part about the girl, Loosie-Goosie, raising up her dress. "That girl's crazy," I finished, "but that's no reason for her daddy to beat her on the head with a boat paddle."

"My stars!" Miss Mary Ann said.

"Had anybody consulted me, I would have warned you not to go out there," Lucas said. He tut-tutted and shook his head. "No place for civilized people. No place at all."

"Well, first thing tomorrow morning, I'm going right down to the courthouse and report him to the child protective people," Biggie said. "That child needs to be taken out of that home."

"Rosebud was ready to put her in the car and take her right then," I said, thinking how glad I was that Biggie wouldn't let him. I'd had more than enough of Miss Loosie-Goosie Baugh for one day.

"That would have been kidnapping," Lucas said. "Now, Biggie, are you sure you want to go poking your nose in something that doesn't concern you? They are ignorant swamp people. They have their ways of raising their young—and they have never been our ways."

"That's right," Miss Mary Ann said. "You really should stay out of it, Biggie."

Mr. Masters nodded, but didn't say anything.

"I'm going," Biggie said. "I have a feeling Annabeth would have wanted me to."

"Could I have another piece of chicken?" I asked.

After supper, Biggie caught up with Brian in the lobby. "Could I have a word with you?" she asked.

Brian looked at his watch. "I have to meet someone at seven," he said.

"This won't take a minute." Biggie led him into the little side room where we had met with the sheriff. I followed.

"Son," Biggie said after we had all taken a seat, "there's a young lady in this town who needs your help."

Brian looked surprised. I guess he had been expecting Biggie to ask him about the murder. "Ma'am?"

"Are you religious at all?"

Now, Brian looked really surprised, and I guess I did, too. Biggie doesn't usually talk that way.

"I guess," he said, embarrassed. "Why?"

"Because, if you are, maybe you feel a sense of responsibility for your fellow human beings."

"Well . . . sure," Brian said.

"Then you wouldn't mind helping one of God's creatures who is sorely in need of a friend?"

"You mean that kid? Annabeth's sister? Sure. What can I do?"

"No, I don't mean Lucy; I mean Emily Faye."

Brian looked away. "No, ma'am. No way. I'm not having anything to do with her." He brushed back his hair with his hand. "If you knew what I know about her. . . ."

"We do," Biggie said. "We saw her out at the bait shop this afternoon."

Brian let out a sigh. "Well, then, Miss Biggie, if you know what she is, what makes you think I could help her—if I wanted to?"

"I betcha I can tell you," I said, surprising myself. "Uh, well . . ."

Biggie looked at me, surprised, but didn't say anything, so I went on. "When I was in third grade, we had a new kid move to town. He was from up north somewhere, and he didn't dress like any of us. He wore *white* Keds to school, and soccer shirts, while all the rest of us wore tee shirts and jeans and high-top basketball shoes. The kids took to calling him 'Miss Jenkins' after a lady who works in the cafeteria and always wears white Keds." I paused and looked at Biggie to see if she'd tell me to shut up. She just nodded for me to go on.

"Not only did he dress funny," I continued, "but he was a loud-mouthed know-it-all—kept bragging all the time about how much better it was back in Ohio where he came from. Everybody hated his guts, even the teachers. Well, one day, I came home from baseball practice, and who should be sitting on my front steps but old Sammy Knudson, that was his name. I like to croaked."

"I had invited him over," Biggie said with a smile.

"Well, I just walked right past him and went up to my room and slammed the door," I said. "Then Biggie came up and told me I had to play with him because his parents were out of town and we were keeping him. Overnight!"

"So, what happened?" Brian said, kind of bored.

I could tell he wanted to get this over with, so I hurried on. "Nothin' much. I went back downstairs and got him off my porch in a hurry, so nobody would see him there. I took him out to the backyard and told him he could throw me a few balls so I could practice batting. He didn't argue, just followed me and commenced tossing balls. Man, could he throw—fast balls, curve balls, grounders. Well, after awhile, I let him bat, and he sent one right over Mrs. Moody's fence and into the next yard. I asked him how come he never told anybody how good he could play, and he said nobody had given him a chance, that they wouldn't even talk to him. I had to admit it; he was right. After that, we got to talking, and it turned out, he was a good guy, just different. I gave him a few pointers on how to dress and how to get along with kids, and before the school year was out, he'd made some friends and the coach had made him alternate pitcher on the baseball team."

I stopped and let out a sigh as Brian looked at his watch. "Well, that was nice of you, J.R., but I guarantee, Emily Faye is not anything like your Sammy. She's poison, and I'm steering clear of her." He looked at Biggie.

"Sorry Miss Biggie. I know you're only trying to help." He left the room and we heard the screen door at the front slam as he left.

Biggie got up and gave me a hug. "You did good, honey," she said.

"It didn't help a bit, Biggie. You saw how he acted."

"Maybe it did. Sometimes, when you plant a seed, it takes a while for it to sprout. Know what I've a notion to do? I've got a notion to examine that little room you told me about. You game?"

"Sure!"

"Then go find Rosebud. I'd like for him to go with us."

Twenty minutes later, we were standing in the court-yard in front of the little door. Rosebud pushed it open, holding the big flashlight he had borrowed again from Miss Mary Ann's sewing basket. He took his big hand and swiped away a cobweb before letting Biggie go in ahead of him. I followed.

"It smells like something has died in here," Biggie said. "Rosebud shine your light in all the corners. It may be a rat."

Rosebud swung the light slowly around the room until it stopped at the pile of old rags I'd seen before.

"Maybe it's another body," I said, surprised that my voice trembled.

Rosebud walked over and kicked at the thing. "Naw," he said, "it ain't nothing but an old blanket. Sure smells though." He spread the blanket out, holding it with two fingers by the corners, and examined it with the light. It was covered with dark stains. "Miss Biggie, I believe this thing's got blood on it."

"Let me see." Biggie walked over and looked. She touched it with one finger. "It's still damp," she said.

"You reckon it's Annabeth's?" I asked. "And if it is, how come it's still wet? It ought to have dried up by now."

"Not necessarily," Biggie said, holding her hand over her nose. "Not in this damp cellar. Rosebud shine the light on the floor—see if there's more blood. Stop right here. What's this?"

Rosebud touched the dark spot she was pointing to and raised his finger to his nose. "Blood," he said.

"Leave everything, and let's get out of here," Biggie said. "I'll report this to the sheriff first thing in the morning."

Once we had left by the little door and were standing in the courtyard, Biggie looked back toward the little door. "My soul," she said. "That door is almost invisible against the brick foundation. It's no wonder the sheriff and his men never saw it."

I saw what she meant. The door was hidden behind a big bush, and the worn paint was almost the same color as the bricks.

"Biggie," I said, "I'll bet whoever killed Annabeth stabbed her in there and then wrapped her in that blanket and moved her to the fountain."

"I'll bet you're one hundred percent right." Biggie rumpled my hair. "Well, there's nothing more we can do here. Let's all go get bathed and into bed. Tomorrow promises to be a busy day."

16

The next morning when I came downstairs, I found Brian, dressed in sweatpants and no shirt, sprawled across a sofa reading a magazine.

I sat down near him and cleared my throat.

He looked up from his magazine. "Oh, hey, J.R."

"I wasn't buttin' in," I said.

"Huh?"

"You know, buttin' in. What I said last night? About Sammy Knudson? It wasn't any of my business."

Brian grinned at me. "Hey, man. No big deal." He went back to reading.

"You should have seen her rubbing up against that guy," I said, glad that Brian seemed to be feeling a little better.

"Um, yeah."

"She sure had me fooled."

"Um-hmmm."

"And you weren't even a little bit surprised?"

Brian put down his magazine and looked straight at me. "Everybody knows about Emily," he said. "All the kids, that is. That's why nobody'll have anything to do with her."

"Those guys out at the bait shop sure didn't feel that way."

"Look, kid, guys, well, you know how guys are— they'll, like, do anything they can—when nobody's looking."

"I'm never going to be that way."

Brian looked at me with a raised eyebrow.

"Well, I'm not!"

"You're young, hotshot. Wait a couple of years, then see what you'll do." He looked out the window with a serious look on his face. "Sometimes life gets complicated. Now, scram and let me read my magazine."

Just then, Biggie came down the stairs with her big black handbag over her arm. "I'm going to the courthouse. I have several people to see, so I may not be back by lunchtime."

"Okay," I said.

"What are you going to do while I'm gone?" she asked.

"I don't know. Hang out with Rosebud, I guess."

"Fine," Biggie said. "Just see you stay out of trouble."

After Biggie left, I went out to the kitchen, where I found Mr. Masters sitting at the table drinking a cup of coffee with Rosebud. Willie Mae was rolling out piecrusts at the counter.

"You mean to say you jumped into alligator-infested

waters to pull the boy out?" Mr. Masters shook his head. "My hat's off to you. Not many men would have had the courage."

Rosebud took out a red bandanna and blew his nose with a loud *honk*, then refolded the hankie and dabbed the end of his nose with it before putting it back in his pocket. "It wasn't what you'd say exactly like that," he said. "See, when that crazy kid commenced slapping that flat-bottom boat against the water, it made a awful racket that scared them 'gators so bad, they hightailed it out of there."

"Wow," I said. "You never told me that part."

Rosebud ignored me and went on talking to Mr. Masters. "Wellsir, quick as a flash, I waded in and grabbed the boy here before they could come back." He pulled a cigar out of his pocket and sniffed it. Willie Mae gave him a look. "I ain't lightin' it, sugar." He grinned, showing his gold teeth. "Of course, they'd a been back, no question about that. All I done was, I taken my window of opportunity, as they say."

I stood up and threw my arms around Rosebud's neck. "Thanks!" I said.

"That there's a mighty peculiar bunch of folks out there." Rosebud was looking at Mr. Masters, who looked away.

"I say, they's mighty peculiar."

"I expect you're right." Mr. Masters looked at his watch. "Well, I'm off. I promised Mary Ann I'd help her hang some new curtains in the Sarah Bernhardt Room. Thanks for the coffee, Miss Willie Mae."

I had an idea. "Hey, Rosebud," I said. "Want to go take a carriage ride around town?"

"You got the ten bucks?"

"Uh-uh."

"Well, then, I'm gonna take me a little nap. Rescuing folks takes it out of a feller." With that, he got up and headed up the stairs.

I watched Willie Mae's back as she worked at the counter. Now she was cutting up peaches to go in the pies she was making.

"I'm about ready to go home," I said, just to make conversation.

"Hand me the cinnamon out of the pantry," Willie Mae said.

I went to the big closet they used for a pantry and found the cinnamon. "Aren't you?" I asked her.

"Aren't I what?"

"Ready to go home."

Willie Mae sprinkled sugar and cinnamon on the peaches piled up in the pie shells. "What would you be doin' if you was home—besides warting me in the kitchen like you doing now?"

I could think of a lot of things, but I didn't really believe Willie Mae expected an answer, so I went outside and sat in one of the rockers in front of the hotel. I watched the tourists dressed in summer shorts and sundresses strolling in and out of the shops across the street. I was mighty tired of being cooped up in this place and was hoping Biggie would solve this case in a hurry so we could go home. I rocked for awhile, just being lazy in the sun. I must have dozed off, because the next thing I remember was Biggie shaking me.

"J.R., wake up. You're going to get sunburned sitting out here. Come inside this minute!"

I rubbed my eyes while I followed Biggie into the lobby. "What time is it?"

"Almost 11:30." Biggie flopped down on the tufted sofa. "I'm roasting. Go in the kitchen and bring me a glass of tea, then I'll tell you what I've been doing."

I brought back the tea, then sat beside Biggie on the sofa. She took a long drink and set the glass on a marble-topped table. "Well," she said. "That hits the spot!"

"Did you talk to the child protective folks?"

"Yep. They're sending somebody out there this very afternoon. They say if things are as bad as all that, they can get an emergency order from the judge and take her right away—today. The caseworker told me she knew a nice young married couple, trained in child psychology. She said she was pretty sure they would be glad to take her."

"Boy, I sure feel sorry for them." I was still mad at that girl for almost getting me killed. "Did you talk to the sheriff?"

"Yep. In fact, there he is, now. He's going to take blood samples from the blanket and also the soil from the floor of the little room. Not much doubt in my mind, it'll be Annabeth's. After that, I stopped by the County Clerk's office and had a little chat with Emily Faye."

"Why, Biggie?"

Biggie decided to be mysterious. "Oh, just girl talk. Afterward, she took her coffee break and we went down to the Style Shoppe. I bought her an outfit and talked to her about the possibility of her going off to college in the fall." She grinned. "Now, let's see if Willie Mae has lunch ready."

After lunch, Biggie announced that she was going to have a nap, but I was to wake her at 2:00 if she wasn't up.

At 2:00, I went to her room and tapped on her door. She was sitting on the bed glancing through her little address book. When she saw me, she dropped it into her purse. "I know who the killer is," she said.

"Who?"

I felt a chill go down my spine when she told me.

"Now, don't you breathe a word to anybody. I'm going, right now, to ask Mary Ann to help me set up a meeting this evening. I want everyone there, including the members of the historical society."

17

Supper was at six. Afterward, we all filed into the lobby to wait for the others. Willie Mae brought in a tray holding two bottles of wine, one white and one red, a bottle of brandy, and a carafe of coffee. She set them on the lobby bar. Rosebud followed with glasses and china coffee cups and saucers. Miss Mary Ann fluttered around nervously, putting out ashtrays and arranging things to her liking. Mr. Masters talked in a low voice to Rosebud, who had taken a seat beside him, while Lucas sat under a floor lamp reading a large book. Brian came in last and sat at the little game table with his magazine. He didn't look at anyone.

The first to arrive were Sheriff Dugger and Deputy Wiggs. They both took seats in straight chairs near the door. The sheriff was still pale, but seemed stronger than he had before. I watched as Deputy Wiggs got out his tape recorder and set it on the table next to him. Biggie walked over to them and they had a conversation, which I couldn't hear, even though I tried.

Next to get there was Hen Lester. She was wearing a royal blue pants suit with a red scarf and a frown on her face. "I hope this won't take long," she said. "I have my study club tonight, and I'm recording secretary."

"Just have a seat, Hen," Biggie said. "I know this is an inconvenience, and I'll make it as short as possible."

Hen walked to the bar, poured herself a cup of coffee, and took a seat on the tufted sofa opposite Rosebud and Mr. Masters. She was no sooner seated than Alice LaRue came in followed by Emily. Emily was wearing a slim straight sundress made of some kind of silky cloth. It was yellow with a design of green leaves and pink flowers. Her hair was pulled back with a yellow ribbon and little ringlets hung down the back and sides. She had sandals on her feet. Everybody stared.

"I don't blame you for looking." Alice flopped down beside Hen. "Don't she look a fright?"

"Not a bit of it," Lucas said. "She's lovely. Just lovely." He got up and offered his chair to Emily, who smiled and took it.

"She certainly is," Hen said.

"It's a waste of money, is what it is," Alice said. "Child's got a whole closet full of perfectly good clothes—mine that I've got too fat for. And now she's talking about going off to school. I don't know what's got into that girl." She talked about Emily like she wasn't even in the room.

"Mama," Emily said, "I'm making my own money,

181

now, and I've got a trust left by my granddaddy. From now on, I'm going to do as I please."

Alice seemed to deflate like this air leaking out of a balloon. She sank back on the couch.

Brian just stared.

Biggie stood in front of the marble fireplace, her head barely reaching the mantel. "Everyone's here, so we can get started. Refreshments are available at the bar. Please, help yourselves."

Alice LaRue was the first there, pouring herself a healthy slug of brandy in a round glass. Lucas had the same while Mary Ann and Mr. Masters had white wine. Hen refilled her coffee cup. Biggie watched while they served themselves. When they had finally settled back down in their chairs, she spoke.

"I have brought you together this evening to reveal the murderer of Annabeth Baugh."

Lucas half-rose out of his chair, then flopped back down.

"Oh, my!" Hen Lester said.

Alice snorted loudly. "Who the hell do you think you are, some kind of Hercules Parrot, or something? We got a perfectly good sheriff to do our sleuthing, thank you, ma'am."

Biggie held up her hand. "As you know, the sheriff had to have emergency surgery, and he asked for my help. He had heard that I've had some success with this sort of thing in the past." She looked at the sheriff, who nodded.

"Well," Hen sniffed, "I still don't see why . . ."

Biggie walked over to the bar and poured herself a

glass of white wine. "Would you like to explain why you were giving Annabeth money?" She looked hard at Hen.

"What? I shall not! That's nobody's business but mine."

"Would you prefer to go down to the jail and explain to the sheriff and his deputy?"

Hen looked at the officers, and looked away quickly. "No, of course not. I'll tell if I must. But it has absolutely nothing to do with that unfortunate girl's death. Nothing!"

"Why don't you just tell us, Miz Lester," the sheriff said softly.

"Oh, all right." Hen switched angrily in her chair and took a breath. "It was because of something that happened long ago, when I was just a girl, before I married Franklin." She looked at Lucas, who had sat up straight in his chair and was glaring at her. She stiffened her back and went on. "Last summer, Annabeth helped me out at home, just light housekeeping is all. I had Honeysuckle coming in once a week to do the heavy stuff. Annabeth just made the beds, loaded the dishwasher, and prepared a light lunch for me and Franklin." She looked at Biggie. "That's my husband. She would go home by one usually."

Miss Mary Ann nodded. "It was because of Hen that I hired Annabeth to come help me here at the hotel."

"Go on," Biggie said.

"Well, one day," Hen went on, "I sent the girl into my bedroom to straighten out my cedar chest where I keep Mama's good linens, old pictures, mementos, that sort of thing. I wanted her to air the linens and re-press them."

"Could you get on with it?" Alice LaRue drained her glass and headed for the bar for a refill.

183

Hen barely glanced at her. "I went in to get some hand lotion and what should I see but that young snoop reading my diary—the one I kept when I was a girl. She looked at me with those big blue eyes of hers and began babbling about how beautifully I expressed my feelings for a certain man that I happened to be in love with at one time. The nerve!"

"And for that, you gave her money?" Lew Masters was dumfounded.

"No, of course not. It was *who* the man was that was a problem." Hen's hand shook as she raised her coffee cup to her mouth. "Oh, I just can't go on. It's too humiliating!"

Biggie went to the sofa and sat beside Hen. "It can't be all that bad, honey. Everyone has something in their past that they're not proud of. Now, go on."

Hen looked trapped, but continued. "You see, he was . . . he was *married*. Oh, my face burns with shame to this day, even though I was only a girl at the time. I wasn't married yet. I hadn't even met Franklin at that time. Why, I must have been—what? Seventeen? Yes, that's it. I'd just graduated from high school and had taken my very first job. I was so proud—to be out in the world, earning my own money."

"That was a long time ago," the sheriff said. "Ancient history. Why would you care if it got out today?"

"Why?" Hen's voice rose. "Because Franklin never knew, you fool. What would you know about propriety, about virtue?" She burst into tears. "F-Franklin thought I was *pure* when he married me. I never wanted him to know otherwise." She stood up and pointed at Lucas. "It was him! That's the villain who stole my innocence."

"This is rubbish. Stop it, right now." Lucas pounded the arm of his chair.

"I have to tell." Hen looked daggers at him. "If I don't, they'll take me down to that nasty jail. It's all your fault, anyway." She turned to Biggie. "I was working for Lucas in his law office. Of course, he was much older than I, and so good-looking. I had a terrible crush on him, and he knew it. The rogue took advantage of me." She paused.

"Go on," Biggie urged.

"Well, one evening, he asked me to stay after hours and help with a case he was working on. . . ."

Biggie put her out of her misery. "I think we can guess the rest. Was she blackmailing you? Annabeth, I mean."

"Oh, no. She just kept talking about how sweet it was. I told her she must never tell a soul and if she kept quiet, I'd give her money from time to time—just to help out because they were so poor and all. She assured me that that wasn't necessary, but I just felt that the money might ensure her silence. That's all there was to it. I only gave her the money to keep her from talking about me all over town."

"You'd be surprised to know how dull the affairs of the older generation are to the young," Biggie said. "She probably never gave it another thought."

Lucas stood up and started for the door. "I don't have to stay here and listen to this."

"That's right, you old fool. Run away. Run away the way you always do when things get sticky." Hen turned to Biggie. "I wasn't the only one. After me, it was Bitsy Weems down at the drugstore, then that little Murphy girl. You thought nobody knew, didn't you Lucas. Well, everybody in town knew about your little peccadilloes, how you liked them young and tender. It wouldn't surprise me to find out you'd been after Annabeth. Maybe you killed her."

Lucas was shaking so much, I thought he'd have a stroke. He sank back into his chair. "You harridan . . . you witch! I'm leaving!"

The sheriff spoke from the back of the room. He didn't stand up. "Before you go, Lawyer Fitzgerald, maybe you'd like to tell us what you were doing prowling around the hotel the night the young lady was killed."

"I couldn't sleep. I was getting some warm milk."

Now, the sheriff got up and stood beside Biggie. "Miss Mary Ann, could you possibly remember whether there was any evidence that anyone had fixed warm milk when you came down to fix breakfast? A dirty pan? Anything like that?"

Miss Mary Ann shook her head. "In fact, we were out of milk." She looked at Lucas. "The milkman always comes at seven. I remember, I'd had Annabeth leave a note for the milkman after supper."

"All right, I'll tell you even though it's nobody's business. I heard *him*," he pointed to Lew Masters, "coming out of his room. Oh, I knew what he was up to. He was going to sneak down to Mary Ann's room."

"Mind me asking what kind of a stake you had in that?" the sheriff asked.

"He's an outsider, a coffin salesman, for God's sake. Mary Ann married into one of the oldest and most distinguished families in this town, the Quincys. My family has looked after the Quincy family affairs for generations. I, well, I feel responsible for her."

"Well, I swear!" Mary Ann said.

Alice LaRue got up and poured herself another brandy. She turned and faced the room, swaying a little on her feet. "What is this, a goddamn fishing expedition? If you know anything, Biggie, spit it out. Otherwise, we'll keep our dirty laundry to ourselves, thank you very much. And as for you, Sheriff, I can have you fired in a blue-eyed minute!"

Emily stood up. "Mama, sit down and shut up!"

I like to dropped my teeth when the old lady, meek as can be, went back to her chair and sat down. Brian looked at Emily with a half-smile on his face.

"You're right, Alice," Biggie said. "I will get to the point. As most of you know, I went out to Caddo Lake yesterday morning to visit with the Baughs. That visit was largely unproductive aside for the fact that I was able to rescue an innocent child who was being badly abused. However, by chance, we happened to stop by the home of a Mr. Hance Johnson, who was able to shed some light on the situation. His family has lived as close neighbors to the Baughs for several generations. Mr. Johnson, himself, is near ninety. He told me that, many years ago, Mrs. Baugh, that would have been Mule Baugh's grandmother, gave birth to a stillborn child. He remembers as a small boy hearing his parents talk about how they buried the child under a cottonwood tree. Days later, his parents said, another infant appeared in the Baugh household, a beautiful golden-haired child who grew up to be Annabeth's grandmother."

"The crazy one," Hen mused.

"That's right," Biggie said. "The crazy one. Only, she

was more retarded than crazy. I did some checking at the courthouse and found that on June 2, 1906, two babies were born in this county, one a stillborn child born to Coralee Baugh, wife of Augustus Baugh. The other born to Rachel Quincy, a girl, Marcella. No father's name is mentioned in the records, and we could find no further reference to anyone named Marcella in the Quincy family after that, no death, no marriage, no probate. It's as if she ceased to exist after her birth."

"Rubbish!" Lucas barked.

Biggie took the little brown book out of her purse and handed it to Lucas. "Your father made payments to Augustus Baugh for eighteen years, Lucas."

"My father had numerous business interests all over the county," Lucas said. "That doesn't mean a thing."

"Maybe so," Biggie said, "but Mr. Johnson said it was common knowledge around there that your father made those payments to the Baughs to keep them quiet about exactly who fathered Rachel Quincy's baby. I wonder if that was why you have always tried to make people believe that crazy Marcella Baugh was the child of Diamond Lucy. Was it to distract them from thinking about her real origins?"

Lucas shut his mouth with a snap and wouldn't say another word. Miss Mary Ann turned white as a sheet, and her voice trembled as she spoke. "It's over, Lucas," she said. "I've got to tell the truth." She looked at Biggie. "Marcella was the child of incest between brother and sister. That's why she was the way she was. It was the shame of the Quincy family. I wasn't supposed to know, but old Grandma Quincy told me about it before she died. Oh, honey." She looked at Brian. "That's why I had to . . . I couldn't . . ."

"You hated the idea of Brian marrying Annabeth. You were terrified of it," Biggie said.

"Mom!" Brian looked stricken. "You killed Annabeth?"

"Honey, no." She got up and walked over to Brian, pleading with him. "You've got to understand . . ."

"It was the blood, wasn't it?" Biggie asked.

Mary Ann hung her head and nodded.

"Miss Biggie," Brian begged, "will you please tell us what this is all about?"

"I'm trying," Biggie said. "It's complicated. Your mother was afraid because Annabeth's grandmother was, in fact, your great aunt. That wouldn't have been so awful except for the fact that she was the child of a brother and sister, both related to you. And somehow, out of this union, came some sort of defective gene, which has caused at least one case of mental retardation in every generation since poor old Marcella Baugh."

"But, how . . . ?"

Biggie spoke patiently. "Years ago, your Grandfather Quincy fathered a baby by his sister, your great-aunt Rachel. We don't know any details, and those who could provide them are dead. All I know is, Lucas's father, old Judge Fitzgerald, in order to avert a scandal, arranged for the baby to be given away—to the Baughs. He arranged payments to be made to the family until the child reached eighteen. That baby was Annabeth's grandmother, who was well known in town as being strange, to say the least."

"Crazy as a bat," Alice mumbled. "I remember once . . ."

"Then, there was Annabeth's uncle, Counce," Biggie went on. "Mr. Johnson told me that he lived in the swamp. Never wore any clothes. It seems the Baughs just turned him out of the house when he was a child. He died of exposure before he was twelve."

"Dreadful." Hen Lester bit her lip.

"They thought this generation would escape the taint until young Lucy was born. She had it, too. It's too bad they live in isolation and ignorance. Today, these children can learn to live happy and productive lives. Anyway, as I said, Mary Ann, you couldn't let Brian and Annabeth marry."

"But I never hurt her. I swear."

"I know you never," Biggie said. "On the night Annabeth died, J.R. thought he heard a ghost in the next room. A man's voice, then a woman crying. At first, I suspected Brian. Maybe they had a tryst in the empty room, then had a quarrel and he killed her. Now, I know who the person was who followed her through the abolitionist's tunnel and killed her with a butcher knife and moved her body to the fountain."

"For God's sake, woman! Tell us who!" Lucas said.

"I'm getting to that," Biggie said. She reached into her big black purse and pulled out Annabeth's little white one and, reaching her hand in, took out the note and passed it to Mary Ann. "Perhaps you would read this aloud for us."

Miss Mary Ann's voice trembled as she read, *Go back where you came from if you know what's good for you. The Angel of Death.* Oh, my!"

"You do recognize the handwriting, don't you?" Biggie said.

Miss Mary Ann nodded.

Biggie went back to her purse and took out her address book, holding it up for the others to see. "If you remember, I asked each of you to sign your names and addresses in my book. I've compared each of your handwriting to that in the letter." She paused and looked around the room, then back at Mary Ann. "J.R. heard voices in the room next door just two nights ago."

"That was Lew and me," Miss Mary Ann said. "We quarreled."

"Why didn't you go out through the door?" I asked. "Instead of the tunnel?"

"I was distraught. I don't know why I did it. He followed me. I just wanted to get away from him." Miss Mary Ann burst into tears. "Brian, honey, you've got to believe me, I never meant for this to happen."

Brian looked away.

Biggie continued to talk to Mary Ann. "You know who wrote that note, don't you?"

Mary Ann nodded.

"You knew that Lew would do anything to make you happy—even murder."

"I—I never asked him to."

"But you couldn't let Brian marry a Baugh."

Mr. Masters never said a word, just sat looking from Biggie to Miss Mary Ann. The sheriff walked over and stood in front of him, then read him his rights, just like they do on television. Mr. Masters looked pleadingly at Miss Mary Ann, who turned her face away, then stuck out his hands for the handcuffs.

18

Home at last! When Rosebud pulled the car into the driveway, I saw my cat, Booger, sitting on the front porch rail, dozing with one eye open. When he heard the car door slam, he sat up and started licking himself like he didn't even notice us. But when I walked over and started petting him, he commenced purring real loud and jumped up on his hind legs so he could rub his face next to mine. After I finished saying hello to Booger, I ran around back and opened the gate to the picket fence that divides our yard from Mrs. Moody's. Sure enough, there was my puppy, Bingo, wiggling all over and peeing on himself because he was so glad to see me. I scooped him up and took him home, ignoring Prissy Moody, who was yapping her head off trying to get all the attention for herself.

That night, after supper, we all sat on the front porch until bedtime.

"There's no place like home," Biggie said. "I'm going to sleep like a baby in my own bed tonight."

I was sitting in the wicker swing. "Me, too," I said. "I want to forget all about that old town."

"Oh, you'll get over it." Biggie watched Booger as he somersaulted across the yard trying to catch a moth. "It's really a charming little town. Anyway, you can't forget just yet. I've invited the Thripps and Butch to dinner tomorrow night. They'll want to know what happened."

I jumped off the swing. "I'm going to call Monica. She'll flip when I tell her about the ghost."

"What ghost?" Rosebud said. "They wasn't no ghost."

I grinned. "She doesn't have to know that."

Rosebud grinned back, showing his gold teeth.

The next night, the Thripps and Butch got there around six for dinner. Miss Julia Lockhart, who writes a column for the paper, had dropped so many hints that Biggie said she could come, too. Willie Mae made pork chops with gravy, fried green tomatoes, purple hull peas, garlic cheese grits, and biscuits.

"I knew all along it was that coffin salesman," Mr. Thripp said. "He had a shifty look in his eye."

"Isn't that just typical of you, Norman?" Miss Mattie spooned gravy on a biscuit. "Always trying to show off. You wouldn't know a clue if it came up and hit you upside the head. Personally, I suspected that Hen Lester, going around like she was Mrs. God, or something."

"Well, come on, Biggie. Tell." Butch squirmed in his chair. "Don't leave out one single thing."

Biggie sipped her tea. "Well, J.R. here provided the

first real clue when he found the notebook that had belonged to old Judge Fitzgerald. Why would he be making payments to the Baughs? They were dirt-poor and couldn't possibly have anything he would want. It just didn't make sense until Hance Johnson told me that he had heard all his life about how "Crazy Ella" Baugh was the child of rich town folks. He knew about the incest, too. It seemed that the Baughs didn't have any better sense than to brag about it and lord it over the neighbors because they had that little bit of money coming in."

"I know people like that," Butch said. "Ruby Muckleroy, for one."

"But how did you find out for sure?" Miss Julia was writing in her little notebook. "Don't seem to me that little book would be enough."

"It wasn't," Biggie said. "I went to the County Clerk's office and looked up the birth records. Frankly, I was afraid the old judge might have pulled strings to keep the birth from being recorded, but there it was, plain as day: a girl baby born to Rachel Quincy, June 2, 1882, father unknown."

"But still, Biggie. How did you know Mary Ann didn't do it? After all, she was the one with the motive. Butch, push those pork chops over this way." Mr. Thripp had already eaten three.

"Well, naturally, she was the perfect suspect." Biggie pushed her plate away and rang the little bell for Willie Mae to come clear the table. "But I just couldn't picture her doing it that way. Poison, maybe, but not stabbing. So I went to see Dr. Littlejohn. He's the only doctor in town and the coroner as well. He told me that it took him and his nurse together to pull the knife out. It had been driven in so hard, it had lodged in a vertebra. Mary Ann would never have had the strength to do that. Then I began to suspect Brian."

"I knew he didn't do it," I said.

"I know you did," Biggie said. "Well, I didn't focus on him very long. After we found the notebook, I began to think Annabeth might have been murdered because of something that happened a long time ago. Those people are stuck in the past. And it seemed strange to me that Lucas Fitzgerald kept putting forth the theory that someone had found Diamond Lucy's baby alive. If that had happened, it would have been a miracle."

"That old man was just a nut about the past," Miss Mattie said. "My lord, who cares about all that? Me, I'm a new-millennium woman. What's for dessert, Willie Mae?"

"Blackberry cobbler." Willie Mae picked up the last of the dishes just as Rosebud came in carrying a tray holding a steaming-hot cobbler and a glass bowl full of whipped cream.

Nobody talked for awhile as we all tasted our dessert. Finally, Butch spoke up. "But how did you figure out it was Lew Masters? Ooh, I got blackberry juice on my shirt. That'll never come out."

"Yes it will," Miss Julia said. "Make you up a paste of baking soda and bleach and leave it on for five minutes—no longer or it'll eat a hole. Then, if the spot don't come out, rub a lemon on it and leave it out in the sun."

Biggie ignored them. "By the back door. After I found out about the incest, I felt that Mary Ann had the most likely motive, but Dr. Littlejohn had already squashed that theory when he told me a small woman could never have plunged the knife in so hard. Brian had no motive. He was obviously head over heels in love with the girl."

"But what about Lucas?" Mr. Thripp said.

"Yeah," I said. "That old man was a lot stronger than he looked."

"Lucas was my prime suspect for a time." Biggie scraped the last of her cobbler off her bowl and put her spoon down. "I thought he might have killed to save the reputation of the Quincys."

"That's crazy," Norman said.

"I think he is a little bit crazy," Biggie said. "At least when it comes to that town. Anyway, after the sheriff got the results of the background check he had run on Lew Masters, my attention turned to him. Turns out, he'd been accused of killing his first wife up in Texarkana. They never could make a case, and he went free. But she was killed with a butcher knife through the heart. It was circumstantial, of course. But that fact, coupled with his obsessive love for Mary Ann, sure made him look suspicious."

"But you didn't *know*, Biggie," Butch said.

"I was pretty sure," Biggie said. "Remember the note we found in Annabeth's purse? Well, I compared the handwriting samples I had gathered in my address book with the writing in the note. It might not hold up in court, but Lew Masters's writing was a perfect match. The sheriff and I thought that was enough for us to try a bluff. It worked and he confessed everything as soon as the sheriff got him down to the jail, so I don't suppose it matters."

Norman Thripp spooned sugar into his coffee. "Was Mary Ann in on it?"

"Oh, no," Biggie said. "She had no idea what he was up to. Mary Ann was scared to death Brian had done it."

"So, Biggie," Miss Julia said. "What did you find out about their historical society? Anything we can use here in Job's Crossing?"

"Yuck!" Miss Mattie said. "As far as I'm concerned, they can keep their old historical society. It's not good to live so much in the past."

"I agree," Biggie said. "I move here and now that we scrap that idea and move on to something more productive. Here's my idea. We fix up the old Claxton Hotel down by the tracks and use it to attract tourists. It could be ten times better than their hotel. All in favor, say *Aye*."

Willie Mae's
Wedding Reception Lane Cake

3¹/₄	cups all-purpose flour	1	tablespoon baking powder
1	cup butter, soft	³/₄	teaspoon salt
1	teaspoon real vanilla	1	cup sweet milk
1¹/₂	cups sugar	8	egg whites

Have your oven heated to 350 degrees. Grease up four round pans and sprinkle on some flour. Cream your butter with your sugar until they be real light and fluffy. Add in your vanilla. Make sure you use the real thing—not that imitation stuff.

Next, mix your flour, baking powder, and salt together and then start adding this to your butter and sugar. Add in your milk, too, but alternate it with the flour. End with flour.

Now, beat up your egg whites 'til they're stiff—real stiff. Fold your egg whites into your batter. Divide the batter into four cake pans.

Bake in the oven for twenty-five minutes or until a broom straw comes out clean when you stick it in the middle.

You can use a toothpick, if you're picky. Cool the layers on a rack while you make your filling.

Filling

½	cup butter	1	cup chopped pecans
1¼	cups sugar	1	cup raisins
8	egg yolks	½	cup candied cherries, chopped
2	tablespoons brandy		
½	cup water	½	cup coconut flakes

Put your butter and your sugar in the top of a double boiler. Don't put it on the fire yet. First, you've got to beat it together then beat in your egg yolks. Stir in your brandy and water. Now, put your pan over boiling water and cook and stir until it's thick. Add in your fruit and nuts. Stir it up good and take it off the heat to cool before you put it between the cake layers.

Icing

1	cup sugar	4	egg whites
½	cup light corn syrup	1	teaspoon vanilla
4	tablespoons water		

Mix your sugar, corn syrup, and water in a saucepan. Put a lid on and let it boil real good on medium heat. Now, take the lid off and boil some more 'til a little dab of it makes a good hard ball in a cup of cold water. If you have a candy thermometer, you can use that. Let it cook to 242 degrees.

Now, while that's boiling, beat up your egg whites until

they're real stiff. Pour your hot syrup *real slow* into your egg whites, beating all the time. Add in the vanilla and keep beating on high speed until it forms stiff peaks.

Spread it on the top and sides of your cake.

This makes a lot of frosting, but J.R. likes it that way.

P.S. Once when I was in a hurry, I used a white cake mix for this. It wasn't too bad.

—Willie Mae